The Fault Mirror

The Fault Mirror

CATHERINE FEARNS

Quill & Crow

The Fault Mirror
By Catherine Fearns
Published by Quill & Crow Publishing House

Edited by Mathew L Reyes, Cassandra Thompson

Cover Design by Fay Lane

Printed in the United States of America

ISBN (ebook) 978-1-967911-03-5

ISBN (print) 978-1-967911-04-2

Library of Congress Control Number Forthcoming

Publisher's Website: www.quillandcrowpublishinghouse.com

To Spiro, Iason, Marie, and Calypso

"Down the gullies of the eras we may catch ourselves looking forward to what will in no time be staring you larrikins on the post-face in that multi-mirror of returning ties, whirled without end to end."

— JAMES JOYCE, *FINNEGANS WAKE*

"At the still point of the turning world. Neither flesh nor fleshless; Neither from nor towards; at the still point, there the dance is…"

— T.S. ELIOT, *BURNT NORTON*

"Tumultuous and universal catastrophes—fires, wars, epidemics—are but a single sorrow, multiplied in many illusory mirrors."

— JORGE LUIS BORGES, *A NEW REFUTATION OF TIME*

CHAPTER 1

Daphne

1980

They walked across the cloudsea, feet caressed by ghosts. Thick morning mist blanketed the low peaks of the pre-Alps, just above the level of the bridge, so that as they traversed the gorge, they had a strange vertigo, as if each next step might send them plummeting into the abyss. On the horizon, Mont Blanc sparkled in a blinding low sun.

An autoroute ran along nearby, but the low drone was just a white noise—too early in the spring for birdsong—and all they heard was the trudging of their boots, the mild pant of their breath, and the jangle of coquilles Saint-Jacques that hung from their rucksacks. The shells marked Daphne and Cyrus Field as hikers following the Way of St. James, and they had enjoyed the friendly enquiries along the route so far. *Yes, we are going all the way to Santiago de Compostela. Yes, we are Catholic.* The novelty of being spotted as pilgrims had not worn off, even if the novelty of being on honeymoon had. Daphne wondered what they would talk about if they didn't have this detour to occupy them.

The insidious smell of sulphur was unmistakable now, and she couldn't tell if it was the tint of her sunglasses or if there was a yellow-greenish tinge to the mist.

"Apparently, there are hot springs within these hills," she said. "It's volcanic. That's why there's no snow." Beneath the attempted enthusiasm, her voice was cracked and hollow.

Cyrus didn't respond, and she wondered if she had said it already. She was nervous in a way she couldn't define. It was impossible to explain to him why this mattered, because she didn't know herself.

For Cyrus, this was an agreed detour to look for a half-remembered place from her childhood, a mild indulgence of his new wife's whim. For her, it was the only reason she was on this pilgrimage. It was everything she had engineered, and possibly the moment she had been waiting for her whole life. His benevolence weighed upon her all the more since she had not told him everything. She had not told him because, if she did, then she would have to articulate a vision that could not be articulated: a castle that had no address, and no public record of ever existing, on the edge of a cliff, in a country she had never visited.

Yet she knew it was there and knew she had been there. That ghostly woman in the shimmering garden—the lace and chiffon, the smile and billowing red hair, like a pre-Raphaelite dream that could not exist outside of a painting—yet it had existed. And most of all, that feeling of overwhelming, all-consuming love that drowned and saved her all at once. Her whole life had been shaped by this yearning, this unspecified urgency. She must find it, and there was nothing beyond.

They reached the middle of the bridge, an Industrial Revolution feat of suspension that combined engineering with whimsy. At each end were twin castle follies, replete with battlements, spiral staircases, and arrow slits. Between them, the main cable curved in a majestic parabola. The bridge spanned a deep river gorge, the exact depth Daphne could not estimate when she gingerly leaned over into the void, because thick mist obscured the bottom. She imagined falling forever. Several bunches of flowers were tied to the railings, because this was the spot for people who wished to fall forever. On either side of the bridge, black cliffs plunged with terrifying verticality, smooth as if shorn, smooth as mirrors. It appeared as if each side of the cliff was reflected in the other, but that could only be a trick of the ethereal morning light, for how could cliffs be mirrors? Bare trees with witch-finger branches fought for position on the odd overhang and belvedere. Into the distance, the cliffs meandered with the river, chaotic, bulging, strata-ed, weeping with the black tears of millennia of drainage. The geological drama was an affront, a provocation. A reminder that their whole lives were nothing but a fleeting moment, less than a blink of God's eye. The horror of it didn't match with the blue skies.

Her low dread rose, as here it came.

"So, where's this house then?" Cyrus put down his rucksack and took out a water flask. "We should be able to see it from here, right?"

Daphne scanned his tone for any sign of irritation or mockery, anything other than that performed earnestness, some cruelty she could use to bitterly console herself later when she would be forced to accept that she was wrong. But she could not be wrong.

Was every big moment of her life destined to be a disappointment? The wedding had solved nothing. She had walked down the aisle, watching herself as if from the outside, telling herself that the nagging feeling was nerves. As she looked into his eyes, the priest before them, and the congregation behind, she wondered if he felt it too, and if they would spend the rest of their lives breaking their own hearts out of fear of breaking each other's.

But she had never doubted that the house would be here, and that it would be the answer to the eternal question that had cast a secret shadow over her life. She had not even thought of a future beyond this point.

"I don't understand. It should be up there."

She squinted at the cliff, shielding her eyes. The white mist and the sun cast an infernal brightness. Everything was blinding, and she couldn't think. He took out the binoculars she'd already grimly suspected would be useless and shook his head as he peered.

"Pretty impossible to build up there. There's hardly any flat ground, and certainly no access. There's a suggestion of a ledge halfway up, but you couldn't climb up to it, and couldn't climb down to it. Must be the wrong location."

"I told you it was on the edge of a precipice," she snapped, making no sense, and she loathed herself for it.

"Look, it's a beautiful place anyway, worth visiting. We're only a few miles from Geneva—let's head to a hotel and do some sightseeing with the rest of the day." He put his arm around her, but she was like a stone. It was all she could do not to flinch. It was not his fault, not his fault. He continued to placate, theorize, and commiserate, but she was already somewhere else, formulating, strategizing. She could not continue to Santiago without finding this castle, the only pilgrimage that mattered to her. She knew he believed it was nothing more than the memory of a dream, and she could not bear to think he was just indulging her in what he perceived was childishness. There was a crack in their foundation, invisible yet splintering their couple as ancient glaciers had splintered this valley, as mirrors cracked incessantly in her dreams.

They hiked on to Geneva with the day irreparably tainted and no ghosts exorcised. Daphne felt little more than a ghost herself as she roleplayed throughout the rest of the day and lay awake long into the night. Eventually, she crept out of bed onto the balcony to look at the view in the cool air. Shivers of moonlight rippled the whole length of the lake. The sky was frighteningly clear, and she could see infinite constellations and the brown-purple, dizzying swirl of the Milky Way. She focused on the shape of Orion and thought with inexplicable sadness that that light was already ancient. Already dead. She was looking back in time as if it were nothing. And if anyone could look at her now from Orion, she would be dead, thousands of years dead and forgotten.

A weather system came in during the early hours, and the next morning, when she looked out over Lake Geneva, there was no blue sky or cloudsea. The clouds were a low gunmetal, and the sky concave, as if a giant cauldron weighed on it from above. Leaving a note—*"Couldn't sleep, gone for a walk, don't wait for breakfast,"*—she stole out from the hotel before Cyrus woke up and hailed a taxi. She knew this would take far longer than even the longest of breakfasts, but all that mattered now was seeing what she knew to be there.

The taxi driver was irritable at such a long journey, and even more irritable at her request for him to wait, but he agreed in faltering English to give her a few minutes. Arriving at the edge of the bridge, she jumped out of the car and almost ran to the same vantage point they had taken the previous day. And her involuntary smile was filled with warmth, because there it was, the house from her memories. Not dreams, not dreams, memories. It was exactly how she remembered it. And yet, how could she remember it when she had never been there?

The smooth, vertical cliff to her right now had a grassy shelf halfway up, on which stood a fairy-tale chateau. It was impossibly grand yet chaotic, its frantic feats of architecture echoing the turmoil of the cliffs and mountains surrounding. An architect had indulged the whim of someone with too much money and too many ideas, but the effect was somehow charming, magical. The building was nestled into a ledge high on the mountain, precariously and purposely close to the edge, which rolled away into the void. The highest tower teetered over it. It was cradled from behind by a concave shield of smooth black cliff, so smooth as to be mirrored. She could see a shadow version of the back of the castle in the cliff. The opposing cliff face was a mirror, so there were infinite houses reflected in each other.

The main white limestone façades had been embellished with powder blue and gold gables and beams, to which had been added two asymmetrical turrets with elongated roofs, a square tower, a horde of smaller spires, and innumerable crenelations. All were woven together by covered spiral staircases. Each storey was cantilevered above the other to give a toppling effect, a pile; each floor a bit uneven and slightly wider than the one beneath it, like an overgrown plant that had shot up from the earth. Daphne couldn't quite define its architectural style. Gothic Revival might be closest. It was romantic yet military, medieval yet modern, austere yet indulgent; no single gaze could take it in. The eye was gloriously bathed in its complexity.

The windows were haphazard kaleidoscopes of stained glass. One stained glass window was much larger than the others, and from her distance, she could not make out the image depicted in the glass, even with binoculars, but somehow she knew what it was—a portrait of the woman with the red hair and flowing dress. Somehow, she also knew the interior of the house was filled with mirrors. She had been inside. In some lifetime.

The garden was a labyrinth of sculptures, fountains, and colonnades, and the grass had overgrown into an alpine meadow ripe for wandering and filled with flowers of every color. A tree-lined avenue of dramatic, wide stone steps led down from the house to...nothing. To the edge of the cliff, where there was no barrier, no fence or wall. A person could roll off the edge gently into infinity.

By adjusting her binoculars, Daphne could make out figures in white moving in the garden, the people of this house of love. They moved like kind wraiths, moved with the slight flicker of an old movie. She could make out few details other than a flame of red hair and a white billowing dress, but she could perceive men and women, and they moved with the ease and confidence of wealth. They seemed to move in slow motion, maybe a trick of the light. The surety of figures that belonged in a painting, a painting brought to life. Her body glowed with unexplained recognition.

The strangest thing about the castle was its belonging. Its

incongruity, the impossibility of its construction, made it so very essential. As if it must have been placed there by some supernatural hand. "Ah, yes, there it is," one would say. "Everything is right with the universe, because there is the house of mirrors." Its impossibility proved its existence. A castle for a strange princess. In the soft gray light, it was exactly how Daphne had pictured it, remembered it, this glorious caricature of peace and joy. It felt like love, like freedom.

She scanned the cliff face for any clue as to how to access the house. From above, it seemed impossible. The cliff behind trapped the house in a concave hollow, with sheer rock face for two hundred meters above. Below, the steep cliff continued for at least five hundred meters down into the gorge. But there was an ascent from beneath, of sorts. People had clearly tried to get up—or to get down. To find the house or to escape from it. A vertical maze of steps rose out of the valley, twisting, turning, breaking off, a multicursal vertical labyrinth. Scraps of ladders, ropes, a puzzle. It was precarious, almost comically so. And how to get down into the valley to make the ascent? Perhaps if she tried from the other side of the gorge, where the cliff was less severe. Or they could walk up the river from some distance away. *They*. Because now she could bring Cyrus back here, show him that she was not crazy, not just holding on to a childish chimera.

The taxi sounded its horn from the edge of the bridge, and she ran toward it, glancing back over her shoulder with longing.

～

That afternoon, a low, somber sun burned as Daphne and Cyrus returned yet again to the bridge. Cyrus's mood was less benevolent now, and he slammed the taxi door with a certain petulance. He said nothing, but she could tell what he was thinking: *A day of their holiday wasted. She was being ridiculous, a child. How much more must he indulge?*

And no house, of course, nothing to see.

The light was different from the morning; the cliffs were nothing but mirrors of each other now, infinite shards reflected in obsidian. The cliffs were absurdly, shockingly smooth, each carved out by some giant scythe. It was beautiful, stark, and mesmerizing, but she could tell Cyrus was not in the mood to appreciate geological oddities. He pulled her into a hug and then led her away. It seemed he was trying to share her disappointment as she looked back towards the cliff, but did she sense a note of triumph too, that he was right?

At that moment, she hated him for his kindness, his forgiveness of her mistake, and most of all for the worry in his face when he looked at her. Because now her memory, or her vision, seemed stupid even to her. She must have imagined it that afternoon, willed it into existence. She must be crazy after all. How could that woman in the binoculars have been wearing such clothes in her lifetime? When had she ever been to Switzerland? All these aspects she had known before, but they hadn't seemed to matter when all this was in her head. The moving image of it had simply always been a part of her, as much as her own limbs.

All of Cyrus's explanations were reasonable. It must have been a dream, a lucid dream, or something she read in a book or saw on television when she was very young and mistook for a memory. He was logical, generous. And yet there was something lost forever between them now, a gulf between them as deep as this gorge. If only he could love her enough to accept, if not to believe. She touched some of the flowers tied to the bridge and understood something of that despair. But not despair quite yet. She knew she would be back, without him, and she knew there was no version of this that would not drive her mad.

CHAPTER 2

Cyrus

"So, there you have it. The Problem of the Disappearing House. It wasn't there, then it was, then it wasn't."

Professor Cyrus Field varied his telling of the story each time, embellishing a detail here and there, adding or removing a little piece of dialogue. But he always followed the telling with a dramatic flourish of his black gown as he moved from lectern to window. Once, his movement had been a sudden trademark dart, an impassioned flurry of almost unhinged energy to rouse the students' minds. Nowadays, it was more of a shuffle.

The seminar room was as much a relic as he was. The top floor of the chapter house, annexed to the college chapel, had been built in the 1500s and changed little in over five hundred years. It was ice cold year-round, and dust gathered in the low vaults where crumbling Protestant whitewash gradually revealed the Catholic frescoes beneath. The only furniture consisted of an old wooden lectern that had once, many centuries before, been a pulpit in the cathedral; two rows of wooden desk-bench structures that students had to slide into awkwardly; and a battered whiteboard on wheels, with its built-in tray of colored marker pens and cloth eraser. The whiteboard was a palimpsest of decades of his scribbles. He kept it partly because he preferred to write things the old-fashioned way, and partly because he knew the students found it quirkily twentieth-century.

The window looked out of the back of the college. He turned away from the students and gazed out across the sea of low morning mist, blanketing the city and pierced by spires. He took a pipe and a silver tobacco box from his tweed pocket and used the window ledge as a table for his ritual, trying to ignore the shake in his hands that was making this process increasingly difficult. Flakes of tobacco spilled onto the windowsill as he tipped and pressed them into his pipe, and he swept them carelessly onto the floor with his fingers. He lit his pipe languidly and looked out across the cloudsea.

He enjoyed the silence of his students deep in thought, as much as he enjoyed the clichéd silhouette that he made, the wistful old professor. He tried to ignore the failing sight that meant he could no longer make out the legions of gargoyles adorning the sandstone spires. Now it was only a general impression of Gothic elegance, with the details filled in by memory. But memory could get you far. Memory was malleable, elastic, molded by desire. If he wanted to embellish the stone figures and grotesques in his mind's eye, make them into something they were not, where was the harm?

Finally, Cyrus turned to the room in a puff of smoke, with the nihilism that ensured no one had ever complained.

"Thoughts?"

He would vary the way he said this, too, because his tone colored the students' responses, and wasn't his life's work to get as many responses as possible? Today, he opted for earnest, approachable, open to ideas. The room was gradually bathed in a tobacco haze as he awaited the first brave soul. Twenty of the world's finest young minds taking Introduction to Philosophy, minds sent to him each year to attempt to solve the unsolvable.

A few tentative hands raised. He knew there would be some prepared answers. Professor Field's Disappearing House Problem was a college legend, and this new crop of young people would have been prepped by the second-year philosophers, just as decades of second-year philosophers had done before them. Last year's group had come in terrified, a couple of them almost in tears, as they had been pranked with the rumor that Cyrus was a tyrant who would have them sent down from the university if they got the answer wrong.

He pointed to a confident-looking boy. He could gauge the confidence by how the boy leaned back in his chair, twirling a pencil. Body language was everything to Cyrus nowadays, since he could no longer make out people's features. Encroaching blindness was bringing out his other senses, making him realize how little he had made use of them before. He guessed this boy was from Eton or similar, most likely.

"She has schizophrenia. The house is in her head."

Never heard that one before.

He scribbled on the whiteboard. The red pen squeaked and ran dry, so he threw it on the floor with the abandon that was part of his act, and picked up a green, inhaling the chemical scent of toxic ink as he removed the lid and poised to write. "Next?"

"He's gaslighting her," said someone. "The house is there, but he refuses to see it and convinces her that she is imagining things."

"Not bad, but since this is a philosophy and not a psychology class, let's go a bit deeper. Clear your minds of preconceptions. What is it they say in those tech companies and consultancies that most of you will end up in? Blue sky thinking. No wrong answers." He winced to himself as he said this, a relic statement of his from seminars past. Seminars from times of hope. They all knew that few of these students would be following their dream careers.

"They're in a movie."

"A computer game."

"It's a drug-induced hallucination."

"A timeslip into a different dimension."

"They're in two different versions of a multiverse."

"It's a hologram."

"*Déjà vu*—past life regression."

"She's been hypnotized."

"He's been hypnotized."

"She made a mistake with the geography. She's mixing memories, conflating the place with another where she had actually been."

"It's entelechy—merely the potential for a house."

"It's a thought-form, a manifestation of the subconscious. Everyone dreams of their perfect house, their fairytale castle. And so everyone sees the house they want to see. Perhaps the guy just doesn't have a dream house."

"It's Aristotle—the paradox of place. If the house has a place, then that place must have a place, ad infinitum—therefore it cannot exist."

"It's a metaphor for the difference between the male and female brain."

"It's a metaphor for the breakdown of a marriage."

"It's a metaphor for the decline of religion—they're on a pilgrimage, and it failed. The holy grail was just a mirage."

"It's a made-up problem by a philosophy professor, an abstraction to make us think."

There was nothing here he hadn't heard a version of before, but he noted everything on the whiteboard and stored it in his mind. He loved the energy, the opening of minds to possibilities, the whirring of cerebral cogs.

"Okay, let's take that last comment, and let's say I made it up. Why? What's the point of this?" As always, he was able to extend their discussion into a fruitful introduction to ontology. The very nature of being: how do we know that anything exists outside of ourselves? How do we know that we exist? Could we be nothing more than someone else's thought experiment, or merely one version of infinite possible universes? What does it mean for a house to exist? What do our interpretations of the problem tell us about ourselves?

They talked of Plato, Hume, Heidegger. It was meandering by design, this first session, to inspire them, free their minds of constraints.

Eventually, there was only one student who hadn't spoken. She had short red hair, not ginger but dyed neon scarlet, shaved on one side, and when Cyrus squinted, he could just about make out the forms of piercings and tattoos. He was about to ask her for a contribution when that annoying Etonian boy raised his hand again and spoke without waiting to be asked.

"Professor, when will you publish the answer?"

"Are you worried I'll die before I reveal it? I'm not planning to croak this semester; don't worry."

I am worried I'll die before I discover it.

Cyrus hated the question because he didn't have an answer,

either to the question or to the problem, even for himself. There had always been time for everything—time to find the answer, time to publish the answer, time to admit he hadn't known the answer before. Now, it seemed time was running out for everyone. The latent terror, a slow vulture circling, was the possibility that there was no answer, and never would be.

"There isn't necessarily an answer. Not every question has an answer. And there are a multitude of truths. Today, one simple question has led us to discuss topics as broad as epistemology, existentialism, Epicurus... Now, who hasn't spoken yet?" He pointed at the red-haired girl. "What about you..." He was about to say "young lady," but one could never be too careful, particularly with his failing eyes. "What do you think about the question?"

She shifted in her chair, and there was a confident pause. "Is it a real-life example?"

Around the room, there were a few draws of breath and a few titters.

"A real-life disappearing house. Love it," laughed the Eton boy.

But there was no trace of sarcasm in the girl's voice. Cyrus folded his arms and put his head to one side, considering. "Why does it matter?"

"I think it matters a lot." She spoke with an international accent he couldn't quite pinpoint, in a voice that faltered but intrigued him with its quiet intelligence. There was a slight defiance to it.

"If this is an abstraction," she continued, nodding slowly to herself as she articulated her thoughts, "then our answers can be philosophical, fantastical. We can explore the realms of impossibility. But if it's a real-life situation, then we must ground our answers in science. In physics, or geology, or psychology. There has to be an explanation."

"Does there? I don't necessarily agree," he said with kindness. "Real life does not preclude the philosophical, the fantastical. If this were a real-life situation, it would not preclude *any* possibility. Because nothing is stranger than real life. What are some of the mysteries of life?" He addressed the whole class now. It was a ridiculous question, but he was tired, and he wanted to see where it took them. There were mentions of dark matter, God, the Big Bang, the possibility of alien life. "Lots of cosmological suggestions, indeed. But before we even get to science, what else?"

"Love," three people said at once.

"Love, indeed. The mysteries of love. Love can make strange things happen. Love can make anything possible."

"Nothing is possible without love…for love puts one in the mood to risk everything." It came like a ghost, a voice from another dimension, this quiet but insistent voice from the red-haired girl.

"Carl Jung," they both said at the same time.

Something happened, some slight shift in the universe. He suddenly wanted to know everything about this girl, and at the same time, he wanted to get away from her as quickly as possible and never see her again.

Dear Carl,

I permit myself to begin addressing you by your first name, now that we are friends rather than doctor and patient. Here in Paris, the World's Fair is in full flow, and if you are steeling yourself for a tedious account of every exhibit, invention, and artwork that I have encountered, you can breathe a sigh of relief. Suffice it to say, the march of progress has reached vertiginous speed, and it fills me with as much dread as wonder. As we shuffled shoulder-to-shoulder through the Hall of Machines, we felt compelled not merely to observe and accept, but to worship these dynamos and diesel engines and telegraphs as some kind of moral force. And I ask myself, what hand is guiding all this? Are we moving toward earthly paradise, or are we poised to unleash hell? All of these things are potential blueprints for a better life. And yet such potential for destruction. Can we live up to these Promethean accomplishments? Because one thing I know for certain is that we are destined to misuse our gifts.

But enough of such dull matters, for I am not here to reveal the secrets of technology, but the secrets of love. My dear Carl, I have fallen helplessly in love, and it is a miracle. Surely, no one in the world can feel the way I do now, and yet I also feel a curious new affinity with every other being in the universe. I have connected to something far more powerful than the human psyche. I have tapped into some collective, subconscious river that runs through the world's veins, that only the lucky few get to experience. And so, I will indulge myself with the sweetness of writing about her, in the hope that it will contribute something to your ongoing study of the mysteries of love.

Imagine, if you will, the Palace of Illusions at midday on Tuesday, June 5, 1900. A momentous day in time. I had already wandered—or battled, to be more accurate, since the crowds were unbearable—through the Palace of Optics and seen the giant telescope and the giant kaleidoscope. My senses were already open to the infinite possibilities of the universe. And then through to the Palace of Illusions. Oh, those mirrors! The exquisite disorientation of it! I have never been fond of mirrors —in fact, I have always avoided them. As you know, I was not blessed with beauty. I am a woman condemned to masculine ugliness, and in my thirty-five years, I have only ever used mirrors as Socrates instructed, to remind me to hide my disgrace through learning.

But in these mirrors, I was distorted and refracted and multiplied. The infinite shards of me sparkled and gave me such hope that tears ran down my face. Yes, Carl, even I—real tears! There were moments when I looked almost beautiful. Time splintered and lacerated; I felt immortal.

And then the room shifted, and the fragments of me turned into fragments of an angel. Some ethereal princess, dressed in white, with blood-red hair and the saddest, kindest eyes I had ever seen. Eyes filled with some primordial knowledge and daring me to discover it for myself. I thought it must be another illusion, some painting brought to life, and I was whirling around open-mouthed, when I collided with the real-life angel. I saw my own soul in those pale green eyes, those endless pools. So fragile she was almost translucent, and yet real, too real. The crowds fell away. She was the world, and the world was her. I felt that every arabesque in that kaleidoscope of mirrors was all the light of the world, focused on that moment just so our hands could meet. Hers were ice cold, like the beginning or the end of the universe. Oh, I could write this romantic nonsense forever—how to explain such a sudden change in the world?

You are probably smiling now, Carl, and imagining with what brilliant, acerbic wit I was able to charm her. I, Lydia Temple, notorious trouser-wearer and seducer of wives. But I'm afraid my brain and tongue failed me, and we stood staring at each other, breathless, until she was ushered away by her disapproving chaperones, looking back at me over her shoulder with longing. Perhaps my reputation precedes me.

I stood, buffeted by crowds, unable to move.

How was the world still turning? How could all these people not have noticed what had just happened? Two souls colliding?

I will not bore you by describing my agony that afternoon at the thought of never seeing her again. Fifty million people have passed through this exhibition, after all—how would I find her? I tried to console myself with the thought that she had been one of the illusions. I wandered through the halls for hours, ignoring the exhibits that had now lost their sheen. There was only one wonder here that interested me, and it was human. On a table display of zoetropes, I found one reel of a dancing girl in a red dress, and I spun it again and again, faster and faster, until I was almost mad with the strobe effect. I imagined that if I stared hard enough at the moving image, the girl would turn into my angel. So I made the girl dance faster and faster, knowing that there was no real passage of time inside the zoetrope, that it was only the illusion of motion. But I felt I should die without that illusion.

I'm afraid to say, Carl, that I became quite frantic—you

know quite well those moods I used to have—slapping at the thing as I spun, cursing it. I must confess that I made rather a scene, and I was eventually moved on by a gendarme.

By the evening, I was in an uncharacteristically subdued mood as I took my usual table at the Folies Bergère. You know we always go there on Fridays—Pauline (who styles herself as Renée Vivien now and refuses to speak English even though I'm not sure her French is any better), Nathalie (who is completely besotted with Pauline although who knows how long that will last), and Liane (who is between gentlemen at the moment).

They were so impossibly glamorous in the latest Poiret dresses with their lace, feathers, and turbans. I was wearing my gentleman's suit—I know you disapprove, but if it was good enough for George Sand, it's good enough for me—and smoking cigars like there was no tomorrow. Because it felt like there wasn't any tomorrow, not without my angel. The claims I have to fitting in among this glamorous crowd are flimsy—my devil-may-care attitude, my large apartment for hosting events… I suppose I am rather good at providing the drugs and alcohol and accompanying people on the piano. Although wealth fits you in anywhere, and I am, after all, the richest woman in this city.

The toast of avant-garde Paris, they call us. They are scandalized, and yet they all turn first to the gossip pages of the Figaro and the Gaulois to read about our latest antics—our extravagant entrances into Maxim's, our affairs with politicians and their wives. They are scandalized, and yet without us there would be no Toulouse Loutrec, for he paints us; or Claude Debussy, for he plays in our salons; or Paul Poiret, for we wear his clothes. We are society's orphans, and scandal is our family.

Pauline's father not only bought up and destroyed every copy of her latest book, but he also had the plates destroyed so it could never be republished. And Nathalie must publish her poems under a pseudonym—there, you see, we have not progressed since George Eliot. Madeleine, the brilliant Dr. Pelletier, only received her medical degree by disguising herself as a man, and she's been blacklisted from practically every hospital in Paris.

In any case, our notoriety stems less from our artistic and scientific talents than from our manner of falling in love. The leading lesbians of the time—it's all the rage, you know, having the audacity to crave sister-love. Indeed, I do feel sorry for the men-loving men, who have it far worse. Not fashionable at all. Liane may still consort with men—the greatest courtesan in Paris, no less—but she survived a brutally cruel husband, and she does what she does to keep her son, so I will not begrudge her anything. You know, the newspapers have started to call us the Amazons, passionate rebels against a woman's lot, full of dreams.

I let Pauline and Nathalie and their latest *faux-amours* witter on around me in our velvet booth, as I stared at nothing, mildly surveying the scene through the haze of tobacco and decadence. We dwell quite happily in this demi-monde, this shadow world where we can shine bright. But there is a fine line between brilliance and boredom, and boredom is a dangerous thing. It is at moments like this that I am tempted to retreat to my chloral hydrate. You cured me so well, Carl, and yet there is always the propensity, I believe. To fall back into fantasy and hysteria.

It was particularly crowded that evening since there was a rumor that Louie Fuller would be dancing. She never announces herself in advance, of course, but all the whispers were of the Serpentine Dance and what costumes and lights she would bring this time.

But there came a moment when the atmosphere felt electric suddenly, some morphic resonance as if I had been charged up by one of those giant dynamos in the Hall of Machines. I knew she was there before I saw her—my angel of illusion. My angel of mirrors. Oh, Carl, I swear to you that I sensed, no, *I knew,* she was about to come in. And then there she was at the top of the main staircase.

She was in a human cage created by her chaperones—two older women, an older man, and another man around her age. Her family, no doubt. She was dressed in the old style—corset, bustle, crinoline. Her dress was a deep red satin, far too dark a color for her complexion, and it clashed with her flaming hair. But a red dress—just like the zoetrope! I felt that I had manifested her from that little time machine after all. Her skin was almost translucent. I could see the blue blood coursing through her. She looked as if she could barely breathe. I watched her eyes widen as she took in the gold and the chandeliers and the flesh. I guessed it was her first time at Les Folies. Her chaperones were as tightly wound up in her as they were in their old-fashioned, stiff clothes, and they began making their way gingerly down the staircase.

"See something you like?"

My friends had noticed me staring and were cackling with laughter. Without taking my eyes off her, I said, "Do you know who they are?"

"The de Valleirys," said Pauline. "Revolution refugees. Lost their estate over a century ago. I recognize them from the Palace of Versailles. I met them there at a dinner once. I heard they were down in the south of France somewhere."

"What are they doing here at the Folies, those relics?" said Nathalie, smoking languidly, feigning disinterest, although I could tell she was looking at the angel too. We have often competed on these matters.

"Some sort of anthropological study?" said Pauline, smoking. "Adventure in Bohemia? They are certainly not here for pleasure. They look positively miserable. I can smell their disapproval from here."

"I imagine they are looking for some new money, and that frail creature Seraphine is the sacrificial lamb."

"Seraphine."

I said it out loud by mistake. It was perfect. A celestial being, of the highest order of angels, of the utmost serenity. And she did glow—not a fiery glow, but a heavenly light.

They moved as one down the staircase, bristling, she a glowing orb encased in rusted metal. My friends prickled with amusement as I stood up.

"Oh, come off it, Lydia. She's half your age and here to find a husband."

"That's never stopped her before. It's all part of the challenge."

And they are correct; in my time, I have seduced the most unlikely candidates. But this was different. There are moments in life when the veil of the future clears; a curtain is drawn back, just for a second, and one realizes that there is no chance about it. One is momentarily placed at an Archimedean point, outside of oneself, outside of time, and one sees the forking paths as clearly as if one could feel the gravel through one's soles, breathe the fresh air. And it is neither chance nor destiny, for the choices become clear.

I could have begun a tortured infatuation from a distance,

lurking about in the shadows of this creature's life, spying on her, clutching at chance moments, snatched exchanges, bathing in sweet misunderstandings and miseries. Or I could have swung around the floor with one of my regulars, to get her attention and make her jealous, performing one of my ostentatious seductions to show her my fabulous unavailability, and then never speak to her in my life. Or there was the path of risk and romance; to declare myself and force the moment to its conclusion. I think you know me well enough, Carl, to guess which path I chose. But I am not so callous as to throw her into the mouth of scandal and gossip solely for my own purposes. I would not have done it had I not been sure, as sure as the sun rises, that she felt the same. Perhaps that sounds arrogant, and perhaps it is, but I saw it in her eyes, Carl. I saw my own reflection come off her face.

I began to move over there, drawn by some invisible thread, powerless to resist even if I had wanted to. My friends' voices called after me.

"I hardly think you are what they…"

"Really, Lydia, you aren't going to…"

Their words dissipated around me, and I was vaguely aware of their raucous laughter as I floated towards the staircase. I had never moved with such purpose in my life, but did I move under my own steam, or was I simply transported over there by fate itself?

She was still inching down the ballroom steps in her precarious heels and tight skirt, supported or caged on either side by —oh, who cares—sisters, mother, governess. What cared I, Miss Lydia Temple, obscenely rich, obscenely American, immune to scandal?

To the delight of my companions, I strode across the floor,

the dancing couples falling away around me into the ether. When I got close up, I could feel her electricity, and indeed the prickling of her companions. Close up, I could see that their clothes were old and faded with loose threads and patches sewn on.

Seraphine wore a gold necklace with a jewelled pendant in the shape of a scarab beetle. The iridescent scarab nestled in the throat of her fragile neck, that neck that should have been destined for the executioner's axe. An heirloom, no doubt. She is trapped with a family of ghosts in this new world, and I will breathe life back into her.

You will ask, Carl, how could I be so sure? I have been infected with the romantic fever ever since I read Baudelaire when I was too young. I am the archetypal lover. But I simply knew the moment I saw her. One knows. I wish that everyone could know. I arrived just as she reached the bottom of the steps, and I presented myself to her with a bow.

And perhaps there is a God after all, because she took my hand and—curtsied!

"Miss Lydia Temple," I said. "I am honored to make your acquaintance, Mademoiselle…?"

"Mademoiselle Seraphine de Valéry. I…like your trousers."

Not the most eloquent of first lines, but let us permit ourselves to imagine that she was as dumbstruck as I. Seraphine! Could it be any more perfect? For she has indeed enchanted me like an angel from the highest orders.

Fortunately, at that stilted moment, we were interrupted by strange lights, new music, and a hush over the crowd. Louie Fuller was coming out to dance. In her diaphanous silk costume and multicoloured lights, she performed her infamous serpentine dance, writhing so that her skirt reflected the light in myriad ways. There was nothing to do but stand side by side and watch. Billowing silks caressed our faces like ghost veils as she moved across the gold disc in the center of the dance floor.

It was mesmerizing.

I had seen it all before, but looking sidelong at Seraphine's delighted face, I was able to experience the wonder again. Oh, to experience wonder again; this is what she has already taught me. She leaned in to me to speak into my ear over the noise. "I should like to dance like that." Her voice was like crystal, shimmering, from another world.

"And I should like to see you dance like that."

At that moment, Louie began beckoning people to join her on the floor, so I took Seraphine's hand, and with a moment's hesitation and a fearful look back at her relatives, she allowed me to lead her onto the gold disc. Well, you can imagine the delighted, outraged whispers as we danced and talked all night. What about her relatives, you may ask? Fortune favors the brave—they were dumbstruck. They retreated to a corner table in the shadows.

Picture it, Carl. Smell her hair and perfume, her reflections in the gold pillars, the wall, and the chandeliers, reflected in her eyes and jewels. The world was a kaleidoscope of lights, and I felt transported onto some higher plane of existence. Gilt and velvet foliage, heady scents of musk and cigar, the white noise of chatter punctuated by shrieks of laughter that made it almost impossible to hear the orchestra. Some waltz by Strauss was playing. But for us, only each other. The world around us spinning, but for us, time stood still.

Around midnight, she was whisked away like the proverbial Cinderella, looking over her shoulder with longing, just as she had earlier that day in the Hall of Mirrors. Sleep was impossible that night, and the next morning, I was counting the hours until I could set off to find her. I pulled up to 52 Faubourg Saint-Germain, the decaying mansion that contained Seraphine. With a juddering of the engine, a cloud of gasoline, and a honk of my horn, I stood to wave from the driver's seat, wearing my driving goggles, ruffled shirt, breeches, and riding boots. I believe I am still the only female driver in Paris, and this is certainly the only Daimler in the city. It seemed there was a disapproving face at every window as the front door was opened not by a maidservant but by Seraphine herself, dressed in a green velvet skirt and jacket and a pale-yellow silk blouse buttoned high at her neck. It was probably fashionable back in the 1880s, and far too warm for the weather, but it accentuated her flame-colored hair perfectly. The scarab sparkled on her chest.

"Your carriage, my lady," I called.

I could see the hint of a reckless streak as she skipped down the steps, and with one wistful backward glance, climbed into the passenger seat. Such courage, to throw her old life away like that. Dash herself against the rocks, just for a chance at love.

We clattered around Paris in the Daimler, making noisy circuits of the Eiffel Tower and the Arc de Triomphe, Seraphine laughing and holding her hat as I took those corners as fast as I could. Then, when we had had enough of driving, we strolled through the Tuileries. We walked in step effortlessly, her gloved hand looped through my right elbow, as I marked time with a cane in my left. The poplar-lined avenues were busy with people on their way to the Exhibition, but we were almost in another dimension, walking through them as if they were ghosts. Or perhaps we were the ghosts. And we talked of everything and nothing.

She is twenty-two; far too young for me, and yet her soul is ancient. Worlds apart, and yet we share so many of the same interests. Same books, same beliefs. We talked of Jules Verne, Maurice Ravel, and Gustav Klimt. Except she is far more political than I. She is all for women's suffrage and workers' rights and is fascinated by theosophy. So closeted has she been that she has done it all by correspondence. While I have been out in society, free yet squandering my freedom on frivolity, she has been locked away studying for a better world. She can teach me about goodness, and I can open these political avenues to her in real life. She loves me, too, Carl. I must have done something good in a previous life to deserve an angel such as this. I can only imagine that our souls were meant for each other. And what on earth could she see in me, other than the fact that we are one?

She is a spiritualist, Carl. And by that, I don't mean one of those Victorian charlatans who profess to communicate with your deceased grandmother by way of a crystal ball. Although, of course, she does meditate. By spiritual, I mean that she can access the astral plane. I don't know what you will think of this, Carl, but she believes in a separate plane of existence, between heaven and earth, which can be accessed by one's spirit, or astral body, which leaves the physical body.

Her eyes are pale emeralds that sparkle with bespoke childishness and mischief. She has a propensity for laughter, even as she talks of death, far too much. "Isn't this life dreadful? I hope it will soon be over." These are the sorts of things she says, so blithe. Perhaps it is her way of coping with poor health; she tires easily, and often her face drains of blood, and she loses her breath.

She is generous to a fault—as we queued for the Ferris wheel, she was giving coins to every urchin that begged for one.

"Why shouldn't they ride? One franc is a whole day's wage to their fathers. My family would have me carried off by some fat old man just to keep them in furs and carriages, while there are children on the street who can barely eat."

"And what would they do if you were carried off by some fat old woman?"

She turned to face me, pained, and I thought perhaps I had offended her by my flippancy. She with her social concerns and me with my flirting. I must confess I had had no idea what a day's wage would be. But she put her hands to my face, her ice-cool white hands, and said, "You are perfectly beautiful. I see it."

Sometimes I feel, Carl, that one beautiful moment can represent all the beauty in the world at once. Seraphine's kindness to the little boy at the Ferris wheel encapsulated all the kindness in the world in one moment. The love I felt when we kissed for the first time—it was all the love in the world, every couple who had ever kissed and who ever will. All their electricity flowing through us at once. Plato, wasn't it, believed in a realm of perfect, unchanging Forms, and that everything we experience in the physical world is just an imperfect copy of those Forms. Well, here is the Form of Love. An archetype. I believe this idea merits further consideration.

Seraphine is constantly giving things away—in the Tuileries, we saw a pretty little girl staring at her, no doubt as mesmerized by her aura as I am. Seraphine knelt down to meet her eyes, cradled her face the way she had mine, and then took off her pearl bracelet and gave it to the little girl. This propensity she has to give away every little thing she owns makes me want to give her the world even more. Seraphine has made me realize I have been living in a bubble, just like one of these giant bubbles at the World's Fair. I believe she could make me a suffragette or a socialist or a knight in shining armor with only a wink of her doe eyelashes. I know you have warned me, Carl, about my impulsivity, but surely in love, everything is permitted.

My crowd of demi-mondaines will make fun of me. I can already hear them. *She will love you as a drowning girl loves the sea; what on earth does she see in the heir to the Temple fortune; she looks half-dead already, like a ghost—or a vampire more like; are you back on the chloral hydrate, Lydia...*

I have always believed that one only has to decide that a day will be perfect for it to be so. But even I could not have dreamt this. It felt like the sun setting on the old world. With the sky a deep violet and the first star already out, I pulled up outside her house feeling both elation at this most perfect day, which I had already anticipated I would relive in my mind all night, and unbearable sadness and frustration that I would now have to release her back to her captors.

Sitting in the car, we both looked down the Avenue Faubourg, where the gas lamps were just coming on for the evening. There was such a force between us, it felt as if the car was in one of those magnetic fields that we saw at the Great Exhibition. This was the moment, and I left it to her. I knew she would do it. I trusted her. She suddenly turned to me with urgency and said, "I will die if I go back. Why go back when I am meant to be with you? We have so little time on this earth, why waste it being afraid?"

And so that was it. I started the engine, took her to Avenue Foch, took her out of that corset, and she will never go back into it.

Imagine the chances. Of all the souls in the universe, I found mine. We have completed each other. Drawn together by forces unseen. I believe that every soul has its counterpart somewhere in the universe, and perhaps the meaning of life is to find that needle in the haystack. Now that the miracle has happened to Seraphine and me, nothing can tear us apart. Her family will try, of course. If she stays here, I will ruin her with my reputation; she is as good as ruined already, in fact. Besides, she is in poor health. Weak lungs and gossamer-thin skin. We will spend the rest of the summer in the Swiss mountains, where she will be restored. She can breathe clean air, and we can be alone to let our passions run unconstrained.

Be happy for me, Carl, and write with news of your practice.

Your affectionate friend,
Lydia

CHAPTER 3

Daphne

1980

The house was there as she knew it would be. Shimmering, little more than a mirage, but unmistakably there. This was real, and now it was the failed visits to the bridge with Cyrus that she knew to be the chimeras, the illusions. Daphne's self-loathing was almost all-consuming. Almost. Because her desperate need to get to the house triumphed over everything. Even her marriage. Their honeymoon was abandoned, and Cyrus was abandoned for now, at least. She loved him, or thought she did, but some invisible, unbreakable thread drew her to this cliff. Any guilt she felt was obscured by the overwhelming gravitational pull of the mountain.

They had got as far as the outskirts of Lyon together before she had stopped abruptly in the road and turned back towards Geneva. By the time Cyrus realized that she was hundreds of meters behind and could barely hear him calling, he was left to either return home or complete the pilgrimage alone. She allowed herself to half-form a resolution that they would salvage things later; at the same time, she had a strange conviction that this replacement pilgrimage might be the last journey she ever took.

Through her binoculars, she saw the white figures flitting in the garden like slow butterflies, and she smiled. But this time, there was another figure, familiar somehow, signalling on the edge of the cliff. Daphne couldn't make out the features or clothes, couldn't see if it was a man or a woman. But they were waving both arms rhythmically. Yes, they were calling to her; they wanted her. Maybe they needed her help.

Daphne crossed the bridge and made her way to the other side of the gorge. The only option was to get to the bottom somehow. The cliff on this side was less monolithic; there were possibilities for descent, and if she could reach the valley floor, she could attempt to climb up to the chateau.

She found a path that seemed to be the way down, but it was blocked by a barrier and a circular sign: Passage Interdit; Danger; Risque d'Effondrement, and with nobody around to tell her otherwise, she interpreted the warning as being for vehicles only. She climbed over the barrier and continued weaving her way gingerly down the slope.

The path was rubble, traces of an old road churned up in places by fallen trees and floods. It advanced in endless, pedantic zigzags, sometimes seeming to lose barely enough height to justify the turn. Every turn took her further from the top but no nearer the bottom, as if the gorge was deepening in real time as she went on. Further into the descent, the forest became thicker and darker until it felt like evening. There was a chill in the air, but when she reached the bottom of the valley, it became suddenly warm, humid. The boxwood forest was covered in a bright green moss that coated the twisted and gnarled trunks. The air felt tropical and smelled of sulphur.

There was no path now, only a river thick and murky with weeds and sediment. Daphne wove her way along its bank, clambering over boulders and tangles of root. As she progressed, the rocks and vegetation appeared to become infused by manmade structures. Some were industrial, breeze block concrete with rusted metal spikes, but others were crumbling Victorian Gothic façades, stucco and pillars, while some toppled Ionic and Doric columns looked positively Roman.

These ruins felt familiar. Daphne passed through the remnants of a nineteenth-century spa, an early hydroelectric dam. She stepped over shards of stained glass and mirror, wove between shafts of cornflower-blue wood planks, exposed beams and cables, and jutting rusted wires. All were covered in lichen and straggling ivy, all eaten away by time. Pockets of fly infestations dotted this Stygian wilderness with infernal buzzing.

Daphne screamed at the reflection of a human skull grinning in a shard of mirror, and gradually she realized that corpses littered the grounds. Some were nothing but skeletons, while other bodies had been strangely semi-preserved by something in the atmosphere. Had these people died trying to get up to the house, or had they fallen from it? Were these bodies centuries, even millennia old, or did they fall recently, within her lifetime? Strangely, it didn't seem to matter. Either way, she felt curious rather than afraid; her horror was only mild. She was among them, and it was as it should be.

Finally, she found the beginnings of the way up the opposing cliff. It was not one staircase but fragments, some made of rope and wood, others carved into the stone. They constantly changed direction as if many different attempts to scale or descend the cliff had resulted in a Piranesian puzzle. The first rungs of the first set of steps were missing, so she hauled herself up by her fingertips. She craned her neck at the vertical labyrinth that lay ahead of her and began the impossible climb; there was no other option. This purgatory of rungs and ledges she had no choice but to conquer. Every step was potentially deadly, but she treated it like a game of chess, one move at a time, always planning. As on the descent, it felt as if each stage was taking her further from the bottom but no nearer the top.

When she took a rest on a vertiginous platform, she looked across at the opposing cliff and saw herself in the mirror. A tiny piece of a huge jigsaw. Her heart lurched in horror at how far she had come and how there was no going back. The only way down now would be to hurl oneself against the rocks.

By the time Daphne neared the ledge where the chateau perched, she had lost all sense of time. She had a vague sense that at some point the sky had been violet, or black, or white; had a vague sense of having been thirsty, hungry, yet was no longer so; a vague sense that days, months, aeons had passed since she had set off from the bottom of the gorge. Or perhaps it had only been minutes.

Her hands finally touched the lowest stone step leading from the house to the edge of the abyss. As she hauled herself up into the garden, and the house loomed behind, something shifted. Some rhythm of its shimmering altered. The people in the garden turned slowly towards her, then froze, their faces locked in…what? Not shock, but a languid curiosity. Even in her confusion, a part of her subconscious realised the enormity of what she had done. She had made a terrible mistake, disturbed something that should never have been disturbed.

A beautiful red-haired woman stood up as if she had seen a ghost.

"It's you. But oh God, why did you come here?"

Dear Carl,

You will think me a foolish, lovesick old woman, but I have done it. I have bought the land and begun to build a castle fit for a princess. But I am already getting ahead of myself.

We spent the most wonderful summer in the pre-Alps, and Seraphine is glowing like a jewel. We avoided the fashionable resorts. Chamonix and St. Moritz are just miniature versions of Paris, and I am no longer interested in skiing and murder mystery parties with Sir Arthur Conan Doyle and his English crowd. I am here for one person only.

Instead, we based ourselves on the lower slopes around the French border near Geneva, where the hikes are easy and the miniaturist drama of crags and belvederes suits our little canvas of love. Unreachable peaks jutted in the background, framing our horizon with the impossible geometry of the high Alps. We stayed in simple guesthouses, occasionally moving on when proprietors realized we were not aunt-and-niece or elder sister-younger sister, but something quite different to each other.

The mountain air has done Seraphine a world of good, and the moderate uplands are perfect for her. Of course, if it were just me, I would climb to those treacherous crags; you know I would. But one thing we cannot choose is who we love. *Yes, we cannot choose who we love.* What a glorious rule—there is one person out there for each of us, we just have to go out searching. If Seraphine could only have fallen for one of those male suitors in Paris who circled her like vultures, her life would have been easier. Not fallen for but settled for, rather. Because most of us settle.

If I could have only settled for another like myself—Natalie, or Pauline, or Liane—life would be easy, filled with meaningless pleasures in our shadow world. Choosing a man would have been even easier. I shall not make you snort with laughter and spill your coffee at the thought of me with one of my aristocratic male English suitors, sniffing out my fortune like bloodhounds on the hunt. Oh yes, I could have been a Duchess or a Lady at the drop of a hat. But the universe intervened.

I can see Seraphine getting stronger here, the color rushing into her like a river, her body no longer frail but lithe, and I want nothing more than this. I wish we could stay here forever. She is like a flower, drooping under the weight of her poppy-blossom head and unsteady hat, with angelic clumsiness. What a pair we are, she with her white ostrich feathers and parasol; me with my top hat and men's boots. Despite her wide-brimmed hat, the sun has warmed and colored her face. She moves quicker and breathes more deeply. She had been suffocating in Paris, like a mermaid out of the sea. Animals die in captivity, no matter how gilded their cages. Seraphine no longer wears that dreadful corset that was crushing her ribs. I removed that instrument of torture on our first night together, and we burned it in the fire. Now she floats in loose linens and silks, with her hair aflame like a dripping candle. She was once a butterfly pinned down and trapped beneath glass, gathering dust. Now she has been released; I have released her, and I am so excited to see what she will do. A ghost coming back to life, like time reversing.

I have never felt so connected to the universe. The blood that flows in my veins is the same as the Alpine water that flows in Les Usses down in the valley. My heartbeat is the same as the rhythmic chirping of crickets. Yet at the same time, all the people and objects around us have faded into the background, and we are on some slightly different plane, some different dimension. Perhaps the astral plane she speaks of is nothing more than this. You will be smiling at my chaotic constellations of metaphors, but I revel in them. I am rather frantic, am I not? But how to put into words such feelings?

On the final day before our planned return to Paris, we climbed a strange mountain called La Mandallaz. It lies at the very end of the Vuache range, a monstrous crease in the earth that runs all the way from Geneva. It was forested all the way up, so that when we reached the top, we gasped with shock at the sudden view of the snowy Alps. The mountaintop was a plateau of flower-deep meadows through which we waded, fields embroidered with color. We walked across a sea of clouds, deep blue above us, and the whole world was turned on its head. We wandered through velvet valleys, rainbow-colored meadows, we tramped through high grasses, whole cities of insects bursting with each step. I caught a golden scarab beetle and trapped it in my hands. Seraphine recoiled at first, and then we marveled together at its iridescent industrial legs and ungainly flight as it took off. It matched perfectly with her scarab brooch. What do you make of these coincidences, Carl? There must be meaning. I say it is a wink from God.

And then we reached a sudden precipice, a sheer drop. We teetered on the edge of it. We had found ourselves above a dramatic river gorge, as if the mountain had been shorn in two by a giant scythe. I was surprised that there was no bridge, but I liked it—we had reached the end of the world. Behind us, the whole of France was laid out, green and rolling, while in front was the blinding white of the Mont Blanc range. The two sides of the gorge like two vast waves, two seas parted in the middle. And indeed, they were waves, back in the days when rocks were molten.

Time moves differently here. I can see time written in the geology, and it tells us that our lives are nothing more than a flash. It was an exquisite feeling, the notion that we were the only two in the world who knew our exact location at that moment. I indulged myself with the fantasy that perhaps nobody before us had ever set foot here. But the strangest thing of all was that we could see ourselves. On the opposing side of the gorge, the cliff was smooth black; obsidian, I imagine, although I'm no expert on geology. It was so smooth as to be a mirror, and we could see the dark reflections of our figures. We waved back at ourselves, our chiral twins. Two more steps forward and we would have plunged into a seemingly endless abyss. Seraphine was delighted, and she danced on the edge like Louie Fuller, rubble tumbling into the void as her feet dislodged it.

"Raphie, please be careful," I called. This reckless streak of hers both thrills me and terrifies me. She called out that she would never be careful again, but she did stop dancing, came close, and held my hands. She looked deep within me with pleading, mischievous eyes, and said: "Let's never go back."

And how I do wish that this could last forever, but it is not for me to hide her away from the world. She looked down into the void and said, "I wish that we could just throw ourselves together." It's more than recklessness; Seraphine has a nihilism about her. I cannot define this fearlessness. What do you think of Nietzsche, Carl? For it is something like that. She is made for death. Not for this world. Well, if she wishes to stay here, her wish is my command, but I will not trap her here like her family has done her whole life. Seraphine will never be in a cage again. I shall bring the Belle Epoque to this clifftop, and you know I will. I don't want her to love me as a drowned person loves the sea. I want to be the air upon which her wings soar. There I go again with my metaphors.

I did some local investigations in the nearest village, and the result is that I have bought the mountain of La Mandallaz. I can picture you smiling from here. *Miss Lydia Temple Buys A Mountain.* The village of Avenières lies about five miles away down the slope, and is little more than a hamlet really, a straggle of farmhouses and cottages with a central square around which is an inn and several small businesses—boulangerie, boucherie, quincaillerie. At the local inn, L'Auberge du Terroir, I found the notary who assisted me with the purchase documents. I must admit it is not entirely clear from whom I am purchasing the land—it may even be common land, and that would explain the amenability of the locals—selling me something they don't own. Or perhaps they were interested in the employment I will be providing, for there will be much to do.

I affected not to speak French, and I overheard various mutterings from the locals in the auberge. About the impossibility of building on the mountain, I ignored—nothing is impossible for Miss Lydia Temple! But there was also mention of earthquakes—apparently, the land lies on a fault. Which is hard to believe, given its green serenity. In any case, the last earthquake here was apparently fifteen thousand years ago, so I shall take my chances. When you love and are loved back, anything is possible.

So, I am now the owner of a precipice which only a lack of vision renders unbuildable. And since my vision is unlimited, I shall build our castle on the edge of the world. I adore fairy stories, and I still have the whimsical spirit of a wide-eyed child. I shall build the house that is the amalgam of every dream and fairytale I have ever loved.

I want to make headway before the first snows, so I have already ordered the limestone, which will be brought to St. Julien by railway, then pulled up the mountain by horse and cart. And I will engage my dear friend Hervé Guimard, whose architecture was always too avant-garde even for Paris, to realize my vision. Some will say it is vulgar. But I adore vulgarity; there is nothing more courageous in these times. I adore turrets, battlements, parapets, gables, finials, stained glass—and so I shall have them all!

Seraphine would prefer something simple, but she indulges me in my excess, because we accept each other for what we are. She has been tasked with the interiors. Rather than trawling the furniture galleries and auction houses of the Left Bank, she is using her mission to get to know the local people. She sets off with her horse and trap, eschewing the use of my Daimler, which languishes useless in a barn. She returns at sunset with a cart full of wobbling chattels—quaint cabinets and tapestries and chests, no doubt purchased for double their worth. She usually brings along some delighted children for the ride. I love to wait for her to come over the horizon. Yesterday, she had a grandfather clock tied upright in the middle of the cart, surrounded by happy children who swung their legs over the sides. Each child was holding a mirror, and the mirrors caught the setting sun so that the cart was like a quivering ball of light.

I instructed Seraphine to source as many mirrors as possible, to fill the ballroom with them in honor of the moment we met. We have quite a pile already, of all shapes, sizes, and ages. I used to be afraid of mirrors. I thought they would reveal a darkness in my soul. But I am no longer afraid of seeing my soul; I don't see it in the mirror, I see it in Seraphine's face.

Nothing great has ever been achieved without the motivation of either love or will to power. I know which I find more beautiful. I insist upon hurling myself against life as if dashing against the rocks. It is folly, of course. But what more romantic way to squander Lydia Temple's fortune than on a temple of love? And the most marvelous thing is this: the house's position is such that no one will be able to see it but ourselves, reflected in the giant mirror on the opposing cliff.

But, if you are beginning to suspect me of locking my princess away in this castle, you would be very much mistaken, for that would be a terrible crime. Her light must be reflected far and wide. This will not be a prison but a sanctuary, and we shall invite other shining lights from across the world. Annie Besant, Marie Curie, Marguerite Durand—they shall all come, and Seraphine shall conduct our séances, and we shall soar together on the astral plane. A house of women, a house of love, our very own little utopia. And you must visit! Men are invited too, as long as they are brilliant, and on the understanding that we desire neither their bodies nor their minds, only their company.

Your affectionate friend,
Lydia

CHAPTER 4

Cyrus

Cyrus waited for the students to leave the seminar room so he could take his time navigating his way down the spiral staircase without any irritating offers of assistance. He then worked his way across the quadrangle, one foot after the other, lamenting the time when he had marched across this grass with urgent pride, his gown flowing, and his head held high. Lamenting the time when there had been all the time in the world. Now it seemed they were all coming to the end.

It was mid-morning, and the quad was dotted with students and academics, but he avoided all eye contact, muttering the students' responses to himself so he could remember what to write down. A flock of magpies, drinking from the fountain in the center of the quadrangle, flew off as he approached. He counted six—what was that, six for gold? In his black gown, he imagined himself as the seventh magpie, taking his treasures back to the nest. *Seven for a secret never to be told.*

He maneuvered past an anti-war protest stall set up outside the door to his building. The students were handing out flyers reading "It's Not Too Late" while recruiting volunteers for various roles in the bunkers. As a protest, it seemed half-hearted, fantasies of resistance belying an entrenched compliance, a giving in to fate. The students politely moved out of Cyrus's way.

Another spiral staircase had to be navigated to reach his rooms on the second floor. They would have to move him to ground-floor accommodation soon. He would have to succumb to using a cane. He was a liability, a fire hazard, a relic. Blind old professor, publishing nothing, peddling the same old lectures. Why did they even keep him? Nobody had asked him to retire, but nobody had asked him not to retire, and the only thing he taught was the Introduction to Philosophy course that nobody else wanted to teach.

When the sirens finally sounded—which they would, for there could be no *if* now—he would not make it to a shelter in time. And in any case, he should leave his place to a young person. That was what the authorities couldn't say. Not all could be saved. Instead, there were subliminal messages everywhere about altruism, doing the right thing, and thinking of your neighbor. It was as if the Rapture, the Day of Judgment, was coming, except they had to judge themselves. The public mood had shifted imperceptibly from denial through the stages of grief, and now, preparing for the apocalypse had become a new way of life. They all did it, if not cheerfully, with a wistful acceptance.

He was exhausted by the time he reached his room. The autumn chill had crept indoors, so he lit a fire in the hearth, cursing himself as he struggled to strike a match. The flames crackled in the grate and reflected in the mirrors around the oak-paneled room, lighting up his thousands of books and the wall of the Disappearing House files.

The files were a fire hazard, but so far he had fended off all attempts to have them consigned to the college archives, just as he had fended off all exhortations to publish on his Disappearing House problem. Or had he been prevented from publishing them? His inner narrative changed according to his mood. In any case, it was all unpublished, and so it sat there, a ticking time bomb of potential ephemerality.

He sat at his desk and began writing up the session notes, the computer-voice narrating as he touch-typed. But he couldn't focus, distracted by something the girl with the shock of scarlet hair had said. Something he couldn't put his finger on.

Cyrus took a framed photo from his desk drawer, a photo of a smiling young couple in hiking gear. He had never been sure why he didn't display it on his desk. Perhaps it gave too much away about the Disappearing House problem. A part of him knew that the students knew it was him. But it was necessary, the outward fiction that it was a philosophical exercise. How could one live otherwise? He could hardly see the photo anymore unless he held it close to his face, but the details were engraved on his mind. When he looked in the mirror now, he still saw himself the way he was then, until he squinted at the lines and unkempt white hair and milky eyes, and he would smile at how the mind plays tricks.

He lit another pipe and had lost himself in contemplation of his photo when there was a knock at the door.

"Come in," he called. He knew it was the red-haired girl before she even entered, but not consciously; it was more subtle than that. It wasn't even a precognition—she was simply expected. *Ah, yes, there she is.*

She stood in the doorway, and they looked at each other for a long time. As if she knew that he had been expecting her, and in turn, she expected him to speak first.

He made a mental note, which he knew he would forget, to look up the phenomenon of morphic resonance. A colleague of his, a professor of chemistry, had destroyed his career with this unprovable theory—a sort of telepathy between organisms, an inherent memory in nature, which explained how dogs know when their owners are coming home, how people sense when they are being stared at. It was like synchronicity—that Jungian notion of meaningful coincidence, except that one thing happens after another. Unfalsifiable. But perhaps everyone was afraid to admit, with their outdated notions of matter, that there might be something in it.

"Hello… You must remind me of your name, Miss…?"

"Haydn. Like the composer. Haydn Young."

She entered awkwardly, but her body language still carried about that strange defiance and self-possession hinted at in the seminar.

"That's a nice name. Very interesting question you asked this morning, Haydn. How can I help you?" He indicated that she should sit down in the chair opposite his desk.

"I think your house is there."

"It isn't." He was surprised at the vehemence in his voice. It was as if they had skipped the first half of a conversation, and yet it felt natural. "I have been there many times. I've combed the area. It has never appeared on any map or satellite image." He felt suddenly tearful, petulant. This was a terrible invasion.

"I think your house is there," she said flatly. "And I don't think it's a philosophy problem."

"Go on." Why did he have this feeling that she knew, she knew?

"It's a physics problem. Your house is in superposition."

The sheer unexpectedness of it hit him like a shockwave. Again, they looked at each other for a long time. He waited for her to elaborate, but she didn't. She looked tiny in the big leather office chair, like a child, almost petulantly swiveling it slightly from side to side with her feet.

"Let's rewind a little, as you've thrown me. Go back to what you said in the seminar," he said. "You think the Disappearing House is a real-life example. How can you be so sure I didn't make it up?"

"Because of these."

She opened her backpack, a ragged military-canvas thing covered in permanent-marker graffiti, and pulled out a document wallet. It was burgundy leather, very old and worn, bulging with yellowed papers and tied together with black leather twine. She placed it carefully on the desk, undid the twine, and opened it, taking out a pile of hand-written letters, well-preserved but clearly aged.

"These are letters from a Miss Lydia Temple to Dr. Carl Jung. They span from 1900 to 1918, and they describe the house from your problem."

Cyrus had a sudden, bizarrely violent urge to hurl the pile of letters into the fireplace and to throw her out of the room. It was nonsense, what she said. Daphne wasn't born until 1955. What could this possibly have to do with her? But even so, for the first time in fifty years, he felt the tingling possibility of an answer. And if there were answers, perhaps he didn't want them.

"I have many questions. First of all, should I know who Lydia Temple is? I've heard of Carl Jung, obviously. In fact, I'm sure I have read his collected letters. But Lydia Temple does not ring a bell."

"No, I don't imagine you would have heard of her. She was an American heiress who built a dream house in Switzerland for her female lover."

Cyrus shrugged his lack of recognition. "Secondly, why do you have these letters in your possession? They look like originals. But I happen to know that Carl Jung's estate is kept in Zurich."

"Not all of it. I'm his great-great niece. Sort of. My parents found these among boxes in our basement."

He sat up straighter in his chair, his credulity still lacking, but his academic interest piqued. "Do you mean to say that these are 'lost' letters? They have never been published?"

"Never published, never recorded, as far as I know."

"Well. That would be quite something, if it were true."

He tentatively picked up a letter and held it close to his face to make out the elegant flourishes of handwriting. The legendary psychologist didn't quite fall within the remit of philosophy, and Cyrus wasn't a competitive man, but he couldn't help circling eagle-like around the possibility of a scholarly discovery, so late in his career.

She stood up again, abruptly, no longer a child but business-like. Surely they were just beginning? But then he realized that she had no intention of discussing it further, preferring to leave him alone with the fallout from her bombshell. She had clearly timed her visit to avoid staying any longer than necessary. "I have a lecture in a few minutes," she said.

"A philosophy first-year student going to a lecture? Stranger things have happened…"

"I'm doing Philosophy and Physics. Dual honors."

"Ah. Hence, the lecture attendance. Hence the superposition?"

Haydn looked unimpressed, no longer interested in talking. "I'll leave the letters with you. Call me when you've read them."

She hurried from the room, as if the letters had somehow become dangerous. He hadn't had a chance to formulate the question—how had she made the connection between these letters and his work? But perhaps reading them would reveal all.

Cyrus relit his pipe. The wisps of smoke fought with dust motes backlit by sunrays through the window behind him, illuminating for a moment an invisible world. The day stretched ahead, with no other teaching or appointments, and there was little to stop him from the indulgence of his armchair by the fire, and these letters. Boredom was a dangerous thing. The door to his bedroom, with its monk-like single bed, was ajar, reminding him that these two rooms and the cold little bathroom down the hall were almost all that was left of his life. He swung his chair around and looked out onto the quad, where he could make out by her hair color the blurred figure of Haydn. She turned and looked over her shoulder up to his window.

You will not believe, my dear Carl, how quickly things have advanced since my last letter. The chateau is already taking shape. If only the world were run by women, how easy everything would be. I told you I was going to enlist Guimard as the architect, but then I realized that all of Paris would be in our business, and that is precisely what I am here to avoid. This house is not to be some famed outpost of the Great Exhibition, but rather a sort of secret society. If you find it, then bravo, you have found it. But do not seek an invitation.

So, I did not enlist Guimard. I had a better idea.

One day, Seraphine and I were sitting on the grass, sketching everything we wanted for our dream house—she the palace turrets and grand reception rooms of her aristocratic past, me the battlements and spires of my indulgent mind—and, of course, the mirrors that have been our signature since the day we met.

"It is a house of women," said Seraphine dreamily. And I realized this house of women should be built by women. So I have found Cécile Butticaz, an engineer from Lausanne, only twenty-four and the first female electrical engineer in Europe, no less. Can you imagine, Carl—a female engineer—and we shall have electric lights! More luxurious even than the Folies Bergère! Cécile understands my vision perfectly—hers is as unconstrained as mine, and the beauty of it is that we are at one with the mountain. We shall leave the mountain as we found it, except with a fairytale castle on top. The cliffs below are alive, crawling with carts that trundle like centipedes. No quarries or steam engines or dynamos—all will be done the old-fashioned way.

Our one concession to technology is that we have dammed part of the river to provide ourselves with power, but we are careful to ensure that the fish can pass via a series of stepped pools. I don't know what the locals of Avenières think of me, but I have certainly provided them with much-needed employment, the women in particular. Cécile prefers to hire women wherever possible and to do the most masculine of jobs. It's wonderful—we have female scaffolders, bricklayers, electricians—the men of the village can only look on in horror and wait patiently for their dinners. Perhaps they will learn to cook their own. And they cannot hate me too much, these men, for I am providing the village with roads and electricity.

I know a thing or two about architecture and engineering myself—as you are aware, my family made their fortune building department stores—so I am heavily involved with the details of the work. I insisted that Cécile engage me as a construction worker. What a lark to don overalls and cap, to push wheelbarrows and unload boulders. Seraphine is not strong enough to do manual labor, but we have discovered that the waters at the bottom of the gorge do wonders for her health. There are sulphuric springs down there. It's a curious smell, not altogether pleasant, and on still days, a green-yellow fog emerges from the gorge. But it's quite medicinal, apparently. And the heat from deep under the earth helps to keep the mountain warm—it will never snow here. So Seraphine has her own private spa resort, five hundred feet beneath us.

She discovered it through her recklessness—she stowed away in one of the baskets we use to winch materials up and down from the gorge. The first time I saw the women hauling her up from there, four of them at the windlass, I ran over in horror—could anything be more dangerous? But then I saw Seraphine swinging in her basket, head and legs dangling over the void, her white bathing dress soaked, see-through, laughing without a care in the world. I began to laugh too, and now I winch her up and down there myself. When I dare to peer over the edge of the cliff during my breaks, I see her at the bottom, a tiny figure, porcelain doll, moving in and out of the water like a nymph.

Now, let me tell you about mirrors. The Hall of Illusions in Paris has nothing on my own Hall of Mirrors. We have filled the main hall with looking glasses sourced from all over. I wanted to forever recreate the moment when I first saw Seraphine, when she was multiplied into infinite angels. But I have placed them haphazardly, so that the effects are constantly surprising. Mirrors of all sizes are placed at random: antique gilt frames, gold and silver, concave and convex looking glasses, a giant chandelier, mirrored floor tiles.

What is this obsession with mirrors, Lydia? That is what you will say. *One too many mirrors. Are you afraid of vampires, Lydia?* But it is just the latest manifestation of my eccentricity. As if the house wasn't eccentric enough.

My one indulgence—ha, all of it is an indulgence—my *greatest* indulgence is the giant stained-glass window. I commissioned it from Jacques Villon, who had it made in Venice, and then it was brought here with a whole train carriage to itself, followed by the biggest cart I could commission, pulled by four horses. The transport costs more than the work. It is in the new style, and depicts Seraphine, of course, as a pre-Raphaelite goddess, all flowing copper hair and cobalt blue dress, limbs draped amid an oak forest.

There is no intentional science in my creation, but the optical effect is quite astounding, mainly due to our greatest mirror of all, the fault mirror. Yes, that's what it is, that smooth cliff opposite—a fault mirror. Cécile explained the geology to me. An earthquake can cause one plate of the Earth to fall suddenly, to slide down alongside the one next to it, revealing a smooth shard of fresh rock, slicing a mountain in two. And because the rock here is obsidian, it is a mirror—a very dark one, but unnervingly clear.

When the light hits the fault mirror at certain times of day, it refracts through Seraphine and turns the mirrors in the house into a kaleidoscope, splitting into a glorious prism of infinite colors. It is otherworldly, like a drug-induced euphoria. But I assure you, no chloral. Those days are over, and all my pleasures are natural.

We have gas lanterns installed, fixed to the walls. And we have electricity, running water, a telephone line. I threw the telephone cable down into the valley myself, as the women cheered. Can you imagine? Who would have thought, only ten years ago, that we could speak to people far away that we cannot see, that we would have light in the dark? It is all a marvel. You set out to create one thing, and you create another, almost as wonderful, in the process. I have said before that I fear the unintended consequences of technology. But the unintended consequences of love are innovation, creation, and beauty. This—this is progress. Sometimes I look at the dark house in the fault mirror, the shadow house, and I dare it to disagree.

Your affectionate friend,
Lydia

CHAPTER 5

Cyrus

2035

He moved through the hall with relative ease towards the High Table. Sight was barely necessary in a place where he had dined almost every night for fifty years. He knew every face of every portrait, every crack in every flagstone, the curvature of every arch and buttress, the way in which gowns draped and candles flickered, reflecting in the glasses and silverware, as the din of confident chatter filled every corner. In First Week, the volume was always greater, effusive young people trying to impress each other. He knew how many steps to take up to the high table without stumbling or feeling, and sat in his usual chair, three down from the Mistress, who sat at the head.

He nodded his usual greetings, then let the talk wash over him for a while as the soup course was served. Blindness was sharpening his other senses, and he found he could distinguish multiple conversations around him. As usual, the talk was of war. Or rather, of the peace talks that only ever seemed to bring war closer. By making bland pronouncements on it, they could somehow distance themselves from it, abstract it into something to be analyzed as an intellectual problem.

Cyrus felt Professor Roy Lightman looking at him diagonally from across the table, preparing to speak. He steeled himself for the inevitable question.

"I say, Cyrus," Roy finally said, in a voice designed for the whole company to hear. "How did the Disappearing House go today? First class of the semester, wasn't it? Any brilliant solutions from the new crop?"

Professor Lightman made the same performance in First Week every year. He was a physics don who had been at the college longer than Cyrus. They were the same age, yet Lightman affected to be younger. He wore slim-fitting, off-white clothes: a white shirt and tie, a cream sweater, white trousers, and a white jacket. His white hair and beard were closely cropped. He only wore his black scholar's gown when compulsory ceremonies required—it ruined the effect. If he had been allowed to wear a white gown, he would have, Cyrus once quipped, back in the days when he could be bothered to quip. Lightman was more like a jazz musician or a preacher than a professor.

A noticeable hush fell around the table, awaiting Cyrus's response. He knew they ridiculed him. And he bore it with the stoicism and detachment of old age.

"As always, it generated interesting discussions about ontology. A good little introduction to philosophy for them, and to their abilities for me. One very interesting student. Name of Haydn Young. Bright red hair."

"Oh? What's her theory?" Lightman didn't look up from his plate.

That it's real, it's real.

"Not so much her theory, but her reasoning. As you know, I prefer questions to answers."

"Professor, you are, as always, as elusive as your house—"

"Perhaps you know this girl, this Haydn? She is doing dual honors, Physics and Philosophy."

"Doesn't ring a bell, no. But as you know, I have over one hundred students…"

And there it was. There always had to be some reminder of Lightman's superiority, even though he was just as much a relic as Cyrus. One could argue that philosophy was pointless, but one could equally argue that physics had brought them all to the point of annihilation. Cyrus replayed their old sparring matches in his mind.

He stopped engaging with Lightman and let the noise envelop him, grateful that the diners to his left and right were engrossed in other conversations. He had spent the whole day reading Haydn's letters. Jung's letters. Lydia's letters. It was a whimsical tale. Poignant, powerful in places, particularly the lively descriptions of the Belle Epoque and its contrast with the horror of what came after. He tried to analyze it as he would any academic source.

The writer was an American, highly educated with a flair for words and indeed a flair for life. Her vivacity was infectious. Her allusions to having been Jung's patient were corroborated by her impulsivity that bordered on mania—sudden grand decisions, excess of feeling, and then, of course, by her eventual descent into madness. And there it was—madness. The whole thing was either a delusion, a fabrication, or perhaps both. A work of fiction. But the key question then became: what was the purpose of this document?

Moreover, what was Haydn's purpose? She seemed so

earnest. Lydia Temple could not be real, and even if she had been real, she'd been mad. Cyrus wondered whether it was an elaborate hoax—but surely they would have left him some breadcrumbs. "They"—this mysterious *they* who would bother to waste their time on him. Because Lydia didn't seem to exist anywhere. He had searched the whole Bodleian database on his computer. If someone wanted him to believe in the letters, they would have inserted some references to Lydia into the recorded history of the world, in places he was likely to find. The fact that she didn't seem to exist at all pointed away from a hoax. But then what? Was Haydn being hoaxed?

The possibilities for Jungian scholarship alone were unimaginable if the letters proved to be genuine. Jung would have been a young doctor in the pre-First World War years, just starting out, and this woman, Lydia, seemed to prefigure all his major ideas.

Something about the letters made him profoundly uncomfortable, even though he was relieved to have decided they were fake. He couldn't define the unease. It wasn't the fact that the chateau was situated exactly where he had been with Daphne— the gorge above Les Usses, the cliff face of La Mandallaz mountain, near the village of Avenières. Or the fact that it fit her description—a fairytale castle with spires, turrets, and blue gables. It was something even deeper than that; it was Lydia's voice, her values. The depth of her love, the generosity of her love, almost chiding him for not being able to love that way himself. Was it the voice of his conscience? The voice of judgment?

Why was this strange girl bringing it to him, and was she clouding or clearing his memories? Haydn tugged at the veil of his self-deception, dragging him into a past he preferred not to revisit, at least not in any personal way. He had taken Daphne's memory and distorted it beyond all recognition. It was no longer human, but a monster, a thing that begot itself. He could not face Daphne becoming real again.

As the evening wore on, he felt more than ever the pointlessness of this charade, this ritual. Dining night after night with the same colleagues, content and wallowing in their superiority. Here they were at the end of the world, exchanging witticisms about Homer and Shakespeare, designed ultimately for no other purpose than to feed their egos. Adding to his unease, he could feel Lightman looking at him and attempting to begin another interminable exchange across the table, one no doubt designed to make Lightman look superior. Cyrus thought he would die if he had to go through the Wednesday rigmarole of after-dinner port and cheese in the Mistress's rooms.

At a sudden burst of laughter across the table over some joke about the catastrophic failure of deterrence, Cyrus stood abruptly, placing his wine glass down so forcefully that it shattered. He hadn't realized how agitated he was until he began speaking.

"This intolerable repartee! What is the point of this high seat of learning, when we all know that morally we have learned nothing? We all knew that deterrence was irrational—we've known for decades—because humans are not rational. A military strategy that doesn't take account of lunatics, good God. Yet we carried on regardless, because we couldn't help ourselves. We sowed the world with dragon's teeth—did we really believe they would stay buried? And now we have lunatics in charge, and we're just waiting to see who is the worst."

As he spoke, he was forced to name to himself the crushing weight that he felt, the crushing weight of the realization of a wasted life. He heard his voice becoming shrill, and he heard that a hush had fallen over the hall.

I must confess that I made rather a scene.

Lydia at the Great Exhibition flashed into his mind.

He felt his neighbor's hand gently on his arm. "It's alright, Cyrus. We all feel the same."

"Yes, yes, I suppose we do. I'm sorry, everybody. Do excuse me, I'm a little under the weather today."

He was saved by the gavel calling for final grace, and after the Latin chant was made, he filed out with the students into the antehall, as the dons squirreled away through the high table door.

He called Haydn from the antehall, his thumbs battling with the numbers on his phone as he was buffeted by students. He couldn't find her on the college voice-activated database, so he struggled and squinted to read the number she had written on the front of the folder of letters.

"Hello?" said a voice giggling at his unknown number.

He felt like a stupid old man when he heard the noise of young people having fun in the background. "It's Professor Field," he shouted, finger over one ear, trying to move to a quieter corner. "Cyrus. I read the letters. I wonder if we might discuss them. Tonight, perhaps."

"Yes, sure." Her voice instantly became serious. "Shall we meet at the Philosophy Faculty?"

He hesitated. The Philosophy Faculty was not far, but it

required crossing several roads in the dark. "Would you mind if we made it the King's Arms? I'm…I'm going blind, you see." He had been shouting over the noise of students, but there was a sudden lull, and his voice seemed too loud. It felt strange to hear those words coming out of his mouth. A few people looked around. It was the first time he had ever said them.

I'm going blind.

"Oh, of course, sorry," she said quickly. "I can come to your rooms then."

There were shrieks of laughter from the phone. Evidently, her friends thought she was talking to some potential lover.

"No, no, King's Arms is fine. It will do me good to get out of college. We have an hour before the curfew." If nothing else, this would give him a change of scenery and test his eyesight in the dark. He marvelled at his own recklessness. Some memory of a spirit of adventure, some spark.

The King's Arms was next door to the college, although it took him several minutes of maneuvering his way down steps, through doors, over pavements.

She was there when he arrived, waiting at the bar. He was grateful for her red hair as he was able to spot her through the crowd. Her appearance was almost designed for a blind man, like a beacon. She half-smiled, more relaxed than she had been that morning, and guided him expertly towards a corner table before heading back to the bar to retrieve two bottles of beer. It was granddaughter-like. He liked the way Haydn dealt with his blindness. No awkwardness, just an unspoken guilelessness. There was a strange naturalness between them, like something unfurling as it should. Almost a *déjà vu.*

"Cheers," she said. "Here you are."

"And here you are." He took from his jacket the folder of letters and placed it on the table between their beers.

She looked at him expectantly.

"It's a wonderful piece of literature, Haydn. Thank you for the afternoon's entertainment. Very well written."

Her expression turned to disappointment. But still, she didn't speak.

"It's a fake, of course." He saw from the way her face fell at his words that she was not the writer of the letters. She believed them to be genuine. He regretted his impudent tone, too harsh, when she was little more than a child.

Haydn regained her composure. "Why do you think they are fake?"

"First and foremost," he said more gently, "because this Lydia Temple didn't exist. The woman seemed to know everyone—according to her, every leading light of the 1900s, every man and his dog turned up to her soirées. But there's no historical record of her."

"No record that you can find."

"No record of her. I do know how to search the internet, you know. I looked her up in the Bodleian database—nothing. It simply isn't credible that someone who claimed to be a close, personal friend of so many writers would not merit a mention by any of them."

"I have an explanation for that."

"Well, before you get to that, there's another, more fundamental problem. Your timeline is all wrong." He hesitated because now he was going to have to mention his wife. "Your house was built in 1900, and it disappeared in 1915. But Daphne—the lady from the Disappearing House problem—was there in 1980. She was…my wife." There. He said it.

Haydn looked utterly unfazed. "You didn't mention the date in your class."

"Not this time, but I do occasionally. And students often ask. If they do, I tell them."

"The chronology is not a problem. Chronology is not relevant. But time is everything. Time is central to the issue. It wouldn't have mattered if you had said 1970, or 1990, or any date."

He was both intrigued and infuriated. How could time not matter? If this were not a fable but a real-life experience, then how could time not matter? Haydn seemed to be referencing some Archimedean point, outside of time. Where had he heard that recently—an Archimedean point? Of course, Lydia had mentioned it in her letters. He shook himself. Haydn was like one of those evangelical Christians who had risen to such prominence recently with their proclamations of the coming Rapture—so kind in their fanatical belief they were right.

It was 11:30 pm. Thirty minutes until curfew. People were preparing to leave, downing their drinks, saying goodbyes. The music had stopped, and the lights were going on. He had been cavalier, venturing out this late, and the sensible thing to do would have been to ask the girl for her arm to help him back to college. But he was irritated with her now. She had made him mention his wife, which he hadn't done in years. This was a fantastical exercise. Was it some elaborate experiment, another joke at his expense? And yet, and yet. Students could be extraordinarily creative. Even if it was a cruel joke, he was intrigued.

"Look, Haydn, you seem to have all this figured out, so I don't know why you need me. Why don't you write an essay on it?"

She ignored the question. "But don't you want to find out what happened to your wife?"

No one had ever dared. Did she have any idea what that question meant? The police and suspicions and the decades of grief and regret and what-ifs, wondering and waiting and blocking it out.

"My wife died in 1980."

"What if she didn't?" There was compassion in her response, but still that quiet insistence. "There's something I need to show you. In the Physics Department."

Cyrus stood up more abruptly than he had meant to for the second time that evening. The half-drunk beer bottles rattled and wobbled. But why shouldn't he be indignant? He was a distinguished professor, she a first-year undergraduate. How dare she run rings around him like this?

"Alright," he sighed. "How about this. If you can prove to me that Lydia Temple existed, then I'll let you show me whatever it is in your Physics Lab."

"Deal."

Dear Carl,

The Chateau des Miroirs—for that is what we are calling it —is now complete. When the scaffolding was removed and taken away, furniture delivered, gardens manicured, servants employed, Seraphine and I had just one day before our first guests were due to arrive. But I believe it will always be the best day of my life. These moments—we must seize them with everything we have and cast decorum into the void!

Let me try to describe these things to you, since you insist on being coy about when you might finally visit us. I cannot even remember the last time I received a letter from you! The chateau is dominated by the main hall; I imagine I was influenced by the vastness of the exhibition halls at the World's Fair. I have filled it with mirrors of every shape, size, and style. As I told you, I placed them haphazardly, with no prior design, because I wish the light to be a surprise every time. And I have included a gold circular disc on the floor, a dominating central staircase, and a giant chandelier. It is just like the Folies Bergère, in fact.

The whole house is a monument to those two wonderful days when we met and fell in love. There is a large round table which is also mirrored—can you imagine the size of the trailer that brought it from Limoges? Alcoves and cornices around the hall display porcelain vases and figures—fragile, delicate, intricate, and beautiful, like Seraphine. The whole place could shatter at any moment. There is a grand piano in the corner, a Steinway, of course, and when I play it, it sounds like ice crystals. I'm sure Debussy will have a fit at the resonance when he comes to perform—no doubt he will demand carpets and curtains to dampen the sound—but I love it like this. It reminds me of Seraphine's crystal voice. Every note echoes to infinity.

I wanted the garden landscaped with vistas and avenues, like the Tuileries, where we walked arm in arm, and where she first held my face in her palms. But Seraphine prefers wild meadows, and no doubt she will let my manicured gardens grow untamed, and no doubt I will let her and love it. I had a grand stone staircase built through the middle of the grass, leading directly from the house to the edge of the cliff. Seraphine insisted on it going right down to the edge of the cliff. I wanted to build some sort of protective barrier, a low wall at the very least, but Seraphine loves the mystery and horror of stairs leading into nowhere. "At any moment we could plunge into the abyss," she said dreamily, as if she were almost wishing for it. So here we are at the edge of the world, and I have never been this happy.

Each bedroom is filled with opulence: velvets and silk and damask—rich, jewel colors. However, Seraphine seems to prefer sleeping on the floor, and I often find her curled up in a corner in the morning, on the other side of the room. I do believe she is allergic to the luxury with which she grew up. I have hired several women from Avenières to do the cooking and cleaning, and Seraphine treats them as friends; she has absolutely no sense of hierarchy, and it's rather wonderful. She is up, tending the kitchen garden in the morning before any of the staff. She has chickens and goats. I do believe she will turn this place into a farm to feed the whole village. She was not born for the upper classes, and I mean that in the best possible way. A princess of a different sort.

That first afternoon, the sky was a deep blue, caressed by wisps of cloud, the greens so verdant they were almost fluorescent. Seraphine and I walked down the grand stone staircase like the king and queen of our own secret land, watched in the black mirror by the shadow versions of ourselves. I sat on the bottom stair, leaning back against a plinth. Seraphine sat next to me, holding my hand, dangling her legs over the void, and we just smiled at each other. She leaned back, and our hands gently prised apart like the painting in the Sistine Chapel, then she backed away to dance on the grass—for me, for herself, for the universe.

There is a dizziness that comes with being this free, so free and loved that one does not fear to dance on the edge of the abyss. The air was heady with high summer. And Seraphine had music to accompany her—the melody was birdsong, the rhythm was the incessant buzz of insects, punctuated by the caws of circling magpies and the tinkle of her laughter. She balanced on the rocks, and the profound risk of it all made everything even more beautiful.

We had our first gathering last night, and I do pride myself on the eclectic bunch I put together. Not for me the genteel political salons of Paris, no Zola or Jaurès or Durand. Leave them to perch upright upon sofas, nodding and smiling. Give me lovers and dancers and potent scents and sensuality.

Picture the scene: I had Pauline, Nathalie, and Liane, of course, and they brought their outlandish clothes and avant-garde coattail-riders. Seraphine had no one she could invite from Paris, and I do feel a constant smarting guilt that I have torn her away from her family, no matter how awful they are. Instead, Seraphine invited two couples with whom she has been in correspondence via the Theosophical Society: the Steiners and the Leadbeters.

Of Rudolph Steiner, no doubt you have heard—perhaps you are already acquainted? He is Austrian but quite the toast of German-speaking Switzerland. He speaks perfect French and English as well. He is from a lowly background—the son of domestic servants—but remarkably well educated. A very handsome man, forty years old with piercing dark eyes. I have never met anyone who takes themselves quite so seriously, so you can imagine the twitching of my pursed lips when he told me gravely that he was an "occultist, social reformer, architect, esotericist, and clairvoyant."

And you can imagine the fun that Pauline and Nathalie had planned. They were practically rubbing their hands with glee as they lauded him: "Oh, what a man of talent, this is extraordinary…and what other talents might you have…"

His new wife is called Marie, a German actress. With her, there was more potential for fun and scandal, since she is a self-described interpretive dancer who moved into Rudolph's house while he was still married to his first wife! Quite the determined lady, and by all accounts very in with the upper echelons of the German army. She and Rudolph are the "spiritual advisors" to General Moltke, apparently, and they visit him regularly.

The Leadbeters are a more jovial couple, or at least Charles was, with his sparkling eyes, bushy white beard, and resonant laugh. Mrs. Emma Leadbeter looked rather malarial after all their time in India. Emma wore a Catholic cross around her neck, a gilded Gothic pewter thing. I found it surprising as I'd had these theosophists down as atheists, and for want of conversation, I asked her if she was religious.

"Oh no." Her expression was disparaging. "The word 'God' was invented to designate the unknown cause of those effects which man has either admired or dreaded without understanding them. The real god is the force of nature."

Rather a buttoned-up answer, so I asked her why she wore such a prominent cross.

She tapped it knowingly on her chest. "As a reminder of the power of belief."

Charles is head of the English Society for Psychical Research and the mentee of the "great" Helen Blavatsky. I say "great" in quotations because, as you know, Carl, I am as skeptical of her as I am of the snake charmers and hypnotists of Vaudeville. The so-called Mahatma letters, by which she received her spiritual revelation, have already been exposed as fraud, and I believe she has never set foot in India, yet she carries on regardless. For Seraphine's sake, I kept my counsel and remained open to whatever this Charles Leadbeter had to offer.

Unlike Blavatsky, Charles has been to India, and he brought with him a young man named Krishnamurti, although we are supposed to call him Kumara. He is supposed to be a new mahatma, and the future keeper of the Akashic Records, a lord of Light. He wears all white robes. He's very young and quiet. I'm not sure that Leadbeter hasn't made him up entirely, plucked him from some village like a toy. But the Leadbeters are very proud of him—they introduced him as the Reformer of Ancient Superstitions, Keeper of Knowledge, and Savior of Future Generations. That sort of thing.

So, we have our very own guru, and apparently, it's all the rage in London. I'm certainly fascinated by Hinduism, particularly by the concept of reincarnation, an idea I find deeply appealing. But to my mind, it is the height of crass orientalism to simply treat this chap as some sort of mystic simply because he is from Bengal. I refused to view him as some exotic spectacle; I judged him the same as everyone else.

"Are you really the vehicle of the World Teacher, the coming messiah? How marvelous, darling. Do you think he might come tonight?" Pauline and Nathalie quickly took the young man under their wings, and no doubt had designs on him that had little to do with spirituality.

In the violet evening, we all had champagne in the garden, enjoying the vertigo of the view. As we admired the chateau's reflection in the fault mirror, Mrs. Leadbeter informed us that in the occult, black mirrors are used for scrying—to see the domain of spirits and elementals, and to see the future. I was about to ask her what future she saw in our giant natural mirror when Pauline interrupted: "Darlings, Rudolph over here says he has complete mastery over time!"

Steiner reddened slightly, but only with pride in his abilities.

"Tell them, darling," said Pauline, draping herself next to Steiner on the stone steps.

"Why yes, indeed," He cleared his throat. "With meditation, it is possible for some individuals to access the astral plane, which is a dimension outside of time. From there, one can see the smallest particles of matter, everything that has ever happened, or will happen. The Akashic Records. It's effectively a compendium of all universal events, thoughts, words, emotions, and intent ever to have occurred or to occur."

"How marvelous, my dear," smoked Pauline. "What on earth does it look like?"

"Ah, well, it's really an indescribable sphere of astral light, of infinite reflections. Kumara here will eventually ascend to be one of its Guardians. But only a trained occultist like myself can distinguish between the actual experience and those astral pictures simply created by imagination and desire."

"What a shame, darling, for I have so much imagination and desire." Pauline's almost imperceptible wink at me said everything: how easy it was to charm men, and their wives. She took the disconcerted Marie and Emma by the arms and led them towards the house for dinner. I heard her lurid singsong voice carrying off into the warm still air: "I wonder if we can all become Guardians of these Akashic Records, my dear Kumara. What a lark. I love to wear white. And imagine, darlings, if there were no time, we could stay young forever."

The rest of us lingered to drink our champagne on the edge of the abyss, looking back at the chateau. I told Charles it was a dreadful thought—to stay young forever. Where would we be without the march of time?

We had our backs turned to the fault mirror. I no longer wanted to see our reflection in the fault mirror, now that Mrs. Leadbeter had brought up scrying. I was thoroughly unnerved. I have no wish to see either spirits or the future. I wish to live in this moment, the only time that matters.

As for this Akashic Records nonsense—I know it's a metaphor and all that, but I'm not sure what it says about free will. What do you say, Carl? If everything that will ever happen has already been written down, does that mean everything is meaningless? No, I refuse to believe that. I will live in the moment, and in this moment I feel happy and free.

"Your house is like a thoughtform," said Charles, as we finally made our way back up the steps to the house. "Yes indeed, the Chateau des Miroirs is a thoughtform. I'm currently engaged in writing a book about this very topic with Annie Besant."

He explained that thought-forms are manifestations of our subconscious. They represent the subtle matter of the universe, the world of the mind extruding into the external world, and they represent particular emotions.

"Which emotion does this house represent, then?" I asked Charles, unable to hide my scepticism.

"Love, of course," said Seraphine, taking my arm and putting her head on my shoulder.

"I'm not sure I see the difference between thought-forms as a spiritual concept and the general act of artistic creation, but it's certainly a beautiful notion," I offered.

"Indeed, thought-forms are generally represented in art," Charles said. "Painting, drawing, music. But this chateau is something more. I would go so far as to say that it is a tulpa—a physical manifestation of the imagination. A thought become real."

"Then you are a tulpamancer, Lydia," laughed Seraphine, taking my arm as we walked back towards the house.

"I am no such thing. One might as well say that I conjured you up from my imagination as well."

She was quiet then, and I regretted my flippancy. Her view of the world is no less worthy than mine. Who is to say that I didn't just imagine all this? Lord knows, and you know Carl, that I have been plagued by dangerous fantasies in my life. Perhaps I need you to cure me again. But no, this time, if it isn't real, I don't want to ever be cured.

So, there we were, this strange party of society's misfits. At least twelve of us, and yet we felt too small, seated at that mirrored table in the middle of the vast room.

After the dinner was cleared, I had planned poetry readings, dancing in the mirrors, a piano recital… But Leadbeter and this Kumara took over proceedings entirely. They might have professed to be egalitarian, but they certainly knew how to tell women what was best. The gentlemen stood at the head of the table and gave us beginners an introduction to Theosophy. I can see why Seraphine had to hide her interest in the movement from her family; theosophy is blasphemous to the upper classes in myriad ways, not least because of its egalitarian nature.

The idea is that of Universal Brotherhood—we are all the same. On the physical plane, bodies might appear to be separate and unconnected, but on the higher planes—astral, mental, or spiritual—bodies are connected in very real ways. The men drew analogies from electricity and magnetism to provide some scientific context for these invisible connections between bodies; they described the universe not as a collection of discrete parts, but as one organism, swirling with cosmic energies. Strange, this link between science and spirituality.

But theosophy also lends itself to all manner of so-called radical notions—votes for women, workers' rights, vegetarianism… It's particularly good on love between women, I must say. According to theosophy, God created androgynous souls, equally male and female. Every soul has its counterpart somewhere in the universe, and over many reincarnations, each half seeks the other. When all karmic debt is purged, the two will fuse back together and return to the ultimate. It's beautiful, although I'm not sure where Seraphine and I are supposed to go from here, since we have already found each other.

So, you may ask, why my hesitancy? I, who throw myself into all things wholeheartedly? Why can I not become Lydia

Temple, the theosophist? Well, I'll get to that. In any case, the lecture became rather dull and there was much snorting with laughter and tangled legs under the table from my friends—"When do we get to the orgy?" from Pauline, and so on. The ladies began to smoke opium and were downright badly behaved. I must admit I was as bored as they were, but for Seraphine's sake, I chastized them.

After this, Kumara led us in a meditation, instructing us in the mysterious power of kundalini. He asked us, in his quiet voice with its irresistible Indian accent, to join hands around the table, "empty your minds of all earthly thoughts, and direct the whole force of your being towards the highest spiritual ideal we know." For me, that was easy—I just thought of Seraphine. "And soon you will see new worlds opening up behind your eyes," he promised.

It was rather like a séance in reverse. You know those spiritualist séances that are rather out of fashion now, very Victorian, where we all join hands to summon people back from the spirit world? Well, this was rather the opposite, the idea being to enter the spirit world ourselves. Instead of the red velvet curtains of a Madame Kozlowska, we had mirrors. Candles reflected in them like a million angels.

I felt nothing, and at one point, I dared to open one eye. I'm sure I caught Steiner quickly closing his eyes, as if he had been watching everyone. I don't trust him. There's no chance he went to the astral plane. He was right there in the room, surveying everyone the way I did. Pauline and Nathalie were well gone, in another world completely, although that was more likely the opium than anything truly spiritual. As for the others, I'm not sure if they were transported or just willing themselves to be.

But Seraphine was another matter entirely. Her body was still there, but all that was not flesh had left this world entirely. It gave me a chill, so unnervingly odd was it to see her like that, just a body without a soul. It was like she was dead. So much so that at one moment, I dashed over and took a mirror from the wall and held it to her mouth to check for the faint mist of her breath. Seraphine is always so very close to death. She almost courts it. A wraith, even now that the blood has run back into her veins. I could only watch, helpless, as her eyeballs rolled beneath their lids, the rest of her motionless. I held one of her hands throughout, and it was ice cold. Kumara held her other hand, and I wondered if they were up there together. Occasionally, her mouth twitched into a smile or grimace, and I wondered what she was seeing: heaven or hell.

In the early hours of this morning, we lay facing each other in bed, fingers lightly touching. I tried to ask her about the experience, but she struggled to explain. She was reticent; not unwilling exactly, but unable. I simply couldn't picture it. Apparently, when you are up there, in the astral plane, you are suspended by a silver thread, and you have to want to come back, to remember to come back.

"It sounds so wonderful," I said. "I wonder why you chose to return."

"I came back to you."

I am worried that one day she won't come back from the astral plane. I imagine hauling her back on her silver thread, just as I hauled her up with the windlass. Except one day she might resist, or the thread might snap.

Is it possible that I, Lydia Temple, feel a pang of jealousy? Not sexual jealousy, for I pride myself on being unsurpassable in that department. Nor physical jealousy—of Kumara, I mean

—for this chap is hardly a catch, even as men go. Nor spiritual, because that sort of ecstasy I am quite capable of attaining here on earth. But I confess, I would love to experience what it's like. I may be able to defy conventions, but I cannot defy dimensions. I am so grounded in the real world. So says the woman who built a fairytale castle.

Carl, I would love to know what you make of all this. Seeing things that aren't there, conjuring things that weren't there before. I have wisps of unease about all manner of things that are happening here. This Rudolph Steiner. Some of his views on politics are downright irresponsible—conspiracies, dark powers, and so on. I'll say more in my next letter. We are on the cusp of a new world, and I fear what it may bring. We cannot hide from it in our little haven. The world is too connected, and it comes to us unbidden. Write to me with your thoughts.

Your affectionate friend,
Lydia

CHAPTER 6

Cyrus

2035

"Why are philosophers interested in the soul? Because of the mind-body problem: how do we bridge the gap between our subjective experiences—feelings, beliefs, desires—and the physical matter of the body? It was Descartes who defined this duality and created the fierce debate that still rages, but philosophers back to ancient Greece and further, eastern philosophers, have debated the existence of the soul."

It was the third seminar of the semester, and Cyrus had already veered from the syllabus. He had a strong feeling that this would be the last time he taught this course—either he would die, or the fragile political limbo in which they currently dwelled would collapse into annihilation—and he felt the pointlessness of it all. The notion of the soul had been on his mind since reading Lydia's letters, and since they were all coming close to death, perhaps it had more relevance than usual. He took the students briefly through the history of "soul speak," from Plato and Aristotle to Kant and Hume, and on to modern thinkers and Eastern philosophy.

He dwelt on Nietzsche for a while, only because the students brought him up. He was back in fashion, Nietzsche, in these nihilistic times. Young people were reading *Thus Spoke Zarathustra* and *Beyond Good and Evil,* trying to find meaning in a world that had gone far beyond meaning. The bleak appeal of nihilism to students nowadays was understandable, and he felt an unbearable sadness for all of them as he peered around the room, taking in the hunched bodies. He thought of Seraphine, who had possessed this Nietzschean nihilism on the cusp of another catastrophe.

"Nietzsche believed in eternal recurrence."

Cyrus moved gingerly away from the lectern, leaving one hand on it to steady himself until he was in front of it. He remembered wistfully the time when this seminar room had been his theater, and he would use every corner of it, swooping his gown over students' heads with a flourish, suddenly darting forward and jabbing his marker pen at people to emphasize a point. Now his physical performance was reduced to pacing to and fro in a defined plane, hands behind his back. "Nietzsche argued that one's self, along with everything composed in the universe, will recur infinitely across time and space. What does that mean, for how we choose to live? Does it mean everything is pointless?"

A girl in the front row raised her hand. "I think it is the opposite." She read from her tablet screen: "Nietzsche wrote in an unpublished note, 'The question which thou wilt have to answer before every deed that thou doest—is this such a deed as I am prepared to perform an incalculable number of times?' So, it makes us want to do our best. Like, the choice you are making right now, is it something you'd be proud to do again?"

Cyrus always felt a chill when this notion came up. He

preferred the idea of reincarnation because it gave second chances. He didn't want to live exactly the same life again—that would be torture. *If you could live your life again…* Yes, he would do everything differently. Perhaps the concept didn't mean the same thing for young people. Or maybe there wasn't much difference between young and old nowadays, as they all approached the end.

"And now we get to science. Has science disproved the soul?" he asked. "The idea of the soul had evolved away from metaphysical notions to ideas rooted in science, language, psychology. Daniel Dennett used new knowledge of neural processes to show that consciousness could be explained without resorting to a soul. Wittgenstein saw the soul as a cultural phenomenon; Quine rejected dualism as lacking in empirical evidence. And yet, and yet. The mysteries of quantum physics offered new possibilities for belief in things we cannot understand. So, what about you, scientists? We have at least one physicist here. Haydn?"

She had been silent since the first week.

"Well, it could be argued," Haydn said in a monotone that Cyrus couldn't interpret, "that quantum physics has given us new cause to believe in the soul. There is an argument that consciousness is quantum. It's called holonomic brain theory. The principles that govern the quantum world are applicable to consciousness. Brain neurons act like a quantum computer, selecting one of the alternative quantum possibilities through the quantum Zeno effect within the synapses. This collapses the wave function, causing a thought to form."

Several students had their hands up, and the Eton boy spoke out first. "But that's unfalsifiable," he said, twirling his pencil. It irritated Cyrus that the boy was looking at him rather than Haydn, but Haydn continued unperturbed.

"At the moment, yes. But it's already been proven that there are quantum effects in biology—bird migration, mitochondria, photosynthesis. And if consciousness is quantum, we can speculate that the soul is quantum. We can also use the theory of quantum entanglement to speculate that souls can be in sync with each other, even across large distances and even times."

"Spooky action at a distance, right?" someone said, pointing at a portrait of Einstein on the wall. The students began a lively digression into the meaning of *spooky*, but Cyrus wanted to stay with Haydn's train of thought.

"Different times? Can you expand?"

"The soul is a form of energy, and due to the law of conservation of energy and information, it doesn't dissipate upon death."

"Are you actually trying to prove reincarnation?" The Eton boy continued to twirl his pen in amused disdain as he looked around the room.

Haydn was unfazed. "Actually, there is an argument that reincarnation can be proven by a person's current existence, using Bayesian probability theory. The idea is this—if the universe is infinite, or at least continually expanding, then what are the chances that you would be alive, right now? Zero. Ergo, you must have been alive before. But anyway…"

Cyrus smiled to himself as she spoke, because Haydn had gone far beyond the understanding of her interlocutor. He could almost hear the cogs whirring in brains around the room. He wasn't sure what she meant either.

"Anyway," she said, "not everything has to have a cause."

Cyrus said, "Ah. That's a bold statement. Can you clarify?"

"Or, I mean… We don't always need to know the cause."

Yes, yes, I need to know the cause. I need to know the cause of her disappearance.

"When you take aspirin, you don't know exactly how it works, right?" she continued. "Like, the biochemistry of it? And then there are things that have causes, but we won't know the cause for a long time. Dark matter, for example. We're still a long way off."

"Maybe we don't want to know the cause of some things," said someone. "God, for example. What will happen when we know the mind of God?"

"Now we're getting into causality, and Hume is for the next seminar."

There was an energy in the room, and Cyrus liked to see young people enthused about something, distracted from the slow-burning horrors of the news. But what would this solve? Cyrus was starting to feel like a dinosaur, teaching obsolete philosophies. Should he have been studying another subject his whole life? He had spent his life asking questions that had no answers. But it was too late to change. The sunk cost fallacy: How many people have wasted their lives on this cowardly premise?

At the end of the lesson, the students filed out, Haydn last in line. He caught himself hoping that she would linger. She did, but only to tell him rather coldly: "I sent you the essay."

"Essay?"

"About Lydia. It will be in your inbox."

She forced a smile and left. When Cyrus entered the quadrangle a few minutes later, he saw her with friends, congregated around the fountain. A boy had his arm around her. It was jarring somehow to see her acting like a normal young person, interacting socially. To him she was like a benevolent angel of death, swinging a scythe and leading him towards his fate.

He walked towards the fountain with his head down, but a flock of magpies flew up as he passed it, flustering him, and Haydn and her friends looked round. Behind them, he saw the white figure of Roy Lightman, striding diagonally across the grass. Meanings circled around him, but what was the universe trying to say?

He found himself moving more quickly than usual, as quickly as his old body and failing eyes would allow, with an urgency to get back to his email inbox. He was breathing heavily by the time he sat down at his desk. And there it was.

From: Haydn Young
Subject: 'On The Existence of Lydia Temple'

He used the computer's voice reader to read the essay out to him. It was either that or magnify the font size to absurd proportions. The computer voice sounded strangely like Haydn's. Most of the Disappearing House files that lined the shelves of his office had not been digitized, and he had a slow-burning terror of the day when he would no longer be able to read them at all.

On the Existence of Lydia Temple, by Haydn Young

In this essay, I will discuss and attempt to calculate the probability of the existence of Miss Lydia Temple, an American living in France and Switzerland in the early part of the twentieth century. I will also posit two further hypotheses: that Lydia Temple was not mentally ill, and that her existence has been strategically removed from history.

Haydn's format and style were classic undergraduate: introduction, argue against, argue for, turn the question around in a clever twisty conclusion. He was used to student flights of intellect, the rhetoric of the privileged, and despite his determined, stubborn scepticism, he decided to read her with the careful neutrality he always tried to bring to his marking.

This essay will present the case for the existence of Lydia Temple. A set of letters exist, purportedly written between 1900 and 1914 from Lydia Temple, an American heiress, to the psychiatrist Carl Jung. She was allegedly a former patient of his who remained in contact with him after the end of her treatment. The letters document her relationship with French aristocrat Séraphine de Valleiry; the chateau they built together on the Swiss border near Geneva, her experiences in the First World War, and her subsequent (apparent) descent into madness.

It has been posited that these letters are fake. It is outside the scope of this essay to examine potential scientific proofs (for example, the paper and ink could be dated), nor is it sufficient to consider the personal narrative testimony (the letters were found amongst the personal effects of Carl Jung by a trusted family member). Rather, in accordance with this as a philosophy assignment, the existence of Lydia Temple will be proven using deductive reasoning.

There are several reasons why these letters have been proposed as fake. Most importantly, there is no historical record of a Lydia Temple. A search of the Bodleian Library database brings up zero records. Internet search engines bring up zero records. Given the vast wealth implied in her letters and the myriad personal connections with significant historical personages (Jung, Nathalie Clifford Barney, Pauline Tarn, Arthur Conan Doyle, Rudolph Steiner, Marie Curie, just to name a few), some of whom were prolific diarists, this is not credible.

There was a Temple family in Pittsburgh, USA, who made their money from the construction industry, but their family records have no mention of a Lydia. Since she mentioned that she had been ostracized from the family due to her homosexuality, this could be explained. There was a Séraphine de Valleiry, but other than her birth recorded in 1878, there is no historical record of her. There is no record of her death, although this was common due to the war and the Spanish flu.

Most difficult to explain is that there is no historical record of the chateau Lydia describes building. This is even less credible given its architectural individuality, the number of famous people listed as having visited, and the well-known architect (Cécile Butticaz) who supposedly built it.

Therefore, it is posited that the letters are fake. But the question then becomes, why? What would be the purpose of such an elaborate, literary hoax?

Could they have been composed by Carl Jung himself,

as a form of hypothetical case study? A simple hand-writing analysis by sight rules out (or makes it highly improbable) that the letters were written either by Jung himself or his wife. Moreover, it was not his methodology to invent case studies—he had stated that this was unethical and unscientific.

Could it be a work of literature? Written by someone else? Then why was it never published? In this case, the principle of Occam's Razor suggests the letters are real, for who would go to such elaborate literary lengths and then never publish?

Since there is no good reason why the letters would be fake, let us imagine for the moment that they are real.

We now return to the question of there being no historical record. This becomes suspicious when we examine the places where we would *expect* to find references to Lydia Temple. As an example, the letters of Nathalie Clifford Barney. According to Lydia Temple, she visited the Chateau in May 1911. Her family archive, available at the Randolph Library, is conspicuously missing several pages from May 1911. Similarly, with the letters and activities of Rudolph Steiner, there are conspicuous and unexplained gaps at the times when he could have been at the Chateau des Miroirs.

A further example concerns the sale of the land on La Mandallaz mountain. There is no record in the Haute Savoie archives of any land sale taking place in 1900. This may be credible for the village of Avenières, and indeed, Lydia mentioned that the villagers may have sold her the land fraudulently, but for the whole region, during a time of such industrial and social change? It implies missing records.

We now turn to the question of whether Lydia Temple was insane. But to assume she was insane is to assume she existed. And if she existed, then the letters are real, and she has been wiped from history. This logic proves three things: that Lydia Temple existed, that she was not insane, and that her existence has been "wiped" strategically.

The question then becomes, why would someone go to the trouble—a vast and comprehensive work—to remove all trace of a person and a building from history? That is a question for the next essay. Further work would also include looking more widely at physical records, casting a wide net—photographs, letters, war documentation. It is feasible to wipe someone or something from digital records, but if we go back to pre-digital times, it becomes more complex.

All these curiosities cannot be a coincidence. It is therefore argued that Lydia Temple did exist, she did all the things mentioned in the letters, and for reasons unknown at this time, her existence was then wiped from history. Indeed, it is her absence that proves her existence.

Cyrus couldn't help but smile at that last sentence. So very Oxford in its opaque promise and deceptive meaninglessness. Almost an aphorism, it was the kind of over-confident bluster that first-class candidates would scribble at the end of their exam, slamming down their pen in delight at their own cleverness. And yet. Haydn had a point. Rudolph Steiner was a prolific diarist, with entries for every day of his adult life, except the weeks he supposedly spent at Chateau des Mirrors.

It wasn't enough to convince Cyrus. And yet, and yet.

"It's compelling, I must admit."

They were back in the King Arms, eating the vegetable pies and chips that Haydn had ordered. He couldn't remember the last time he had had lunch outside of the college refectory, and it felt exotic. Haydn's eyes had lit up at his begrudging interest.

"And a bit scary, right? That someone could have gone to all the trouble of removing her from historical record."

"Hold on. If you're determined to prove a hypothesis, it's convincing. But your hypothesis is flawed because it's based on your *wish* for her to exist. Why is it so important to you that she exists?" He held up his hands, palms down, in a calming motion. "Look, I'm willing to look further into this. But I'm not convinced yet. Very well-written essay, by the way. One possibility you don't mention is the fact that Lydia Temple may have been hallucinating. I know you argue that she was not mad, but she mentions herself several times that she had been addicted to chloral hydrate at one point."

"She may not have been addicted. It was a treatment option for mental illness at that time. Carl Jung may have even prescribed it to her himself."

"Yes, okay, but either way, it is known to be a hallucinogen."

"That's one long and complex hallucination."

They both shrugged.

"Another possibility that you don't mention in your essay is that the hoaxer is…you, Haydn. A rather obvious one, particularly if we're talking about Occam's Razor. What could be simpler than that?" He tried to gauge her reaction to his accusation, but she was impassive as ever.

"You don't trust me?"

"I like you. I'm not sure yet if I trust you."

"But what would be my purpose?"

"I don't know. Students do all sorts of things. Perhaps you're conducting an experiment, or fulfilling a dare, or some sort of immersive theater performance... There's a part of me that feels as if I'm being strung along, led into a trap."

"Maybe." She shrugged. "But sometimes, the only way to know if it is a trap is to walk into it. You know, these letters could change the face of Jung scholarship. So many of his fundamental concepts are proposed by Lydia—archetypes, the shadow self, the anima and animus, collective subconscious, synchronicity..."

"Well, that's all very convenient for feminists, isn't it?"

Haydn bristled. "What do you mean?"

"For me, it renders the text highly suspicious when so many of the notions that underpin modern psychiatry are just casually thrown around by a slightly unhinged woman in her gossipy letter. Conveniently, before Jung came up with them." He had gone a bit too far, and he could see her reddening with offence. What was the matter with him? Why did these letters make him angry?

"You'd rather believe they are fraudulent than entertain the possibility that a woman came up with Jung's ideas? It wouldn't negate any of his work. Ideas must come from somewhere. Jung himself was very complementary, for example, about his own wife's influence on his thought."

Cyrus wished he had not turned the conversation this way.

He had made himself ugly, sneering. "There's something else," he said. "How did you make the connection? With me, I mean?"

Haydn put her head on one side. "You're a well-known philosopher."

"Come off it. I'm not a famous philosopher. Back in the day, perhaps, I was known. But you flatter me. I'm a has-been. The Disappearing House is not a standard problem. I never published on it."

"Yes, but it has been cited in the works of others."

"Hardly. You would not have read those letters and thought, 'Oh, that sounds like it might explain the Disappearing House.' And don't give me synchronicity. It wasn't a coincidence. You may be Jung's great-great-niece, but he can't explain everything."

"I wasn't going to use synchronicity. But I do have an answer. That wasn't part of our deal, though. It will come later. You agreed to come to the Physics Lab."

"We're getting into semantics now. And semantics is for another lecture. But alright."

It will come later.

He was allowing her to lead him on this merry dance, this dance of death, on the edge of the abyss. For where else could it lead but to the edge?

Dear Carl,

How are you, my dear friend? Tell me about your research, your patients. No names, of course, for I know you are a stickler for patient confidentiality. I have no doubt that you have used me as an example or a case study, and I don't mind in the slightest. In fact, the egotist in me rather likes it. We do hope to make a difference, after all. What about this for a title: *Miss Lydia Temple: A Case of American Hysteria Cured By Love.*

You see how I understand myself so very well? I watch myself from some Archimedian point outside of my actions. There she goes again with her blithe self-analysis, insisting on doing your job for you.

Well, time ticks on here. Or does it? It's a curious thing, but sometimes I feel I am losing that most human sense of the forward march of time. Sometimes I feel we are in a timeless place, and I cannot decide if that is bliss or misery. Time feels somehow elastic here. Days pass like lifetimes or moments. What do I mean by that? I mean that, if we had all the time in the world, there would be no more striving, no more yearning. And where would we be without yearning? Without the urgency of mortality, we would stagnate. Time would become not a gift but a burden. But it is more than that. For they weren't *happy*, were they, the lotus eaters? There was always supposed to be something dark about the lotus eaters. A terrible complacency as the decline set in around them.

We are surrounded by space, time, and death for a reason—

otherwise, we would not give our actions the same importance. It is the very limited nature of life, the fleetingness, that makes it so precious. That is why I try to seize moments—those moments would be meaningless if they were infinite. When I look up at the stars, I know I am looking at light from things that are already long dead. And perhaps we are already as good as dead, even as we dance in our finery.

What I am trying to tell you is that being here has distorted my sense of time out of all proportion. Some days, I cannot recall what happened the evening before, while childhood memories suddenly burst forth uninvited—things long forgotten. It seems a lifetime ago that I built this house, as if we have always been here, and yet I remember every second of that day with Seraphine in the Tuileries as if it were yesterday.

I imagine it is partly the disorientation of people coming and going. The guest list seems to have taken on a life of its own; strangers arrive unbidden like memories. Sometimes, I feel that the house itself invited them, drew them in magnetically.

Seraphine loves the idea of communal living. I thought I was the free-spirited one until I met her. She abhors private property, espousing Tolstoyan values of passive resistance to evil through non-violent means, vegetarianism, that sort of thing. And it's all very well, I suppose, building a co-operative system, sowing the seeds of a utopia.

So, people come and go like ghosts. Myself, Seraphine, and the house are the only constants. No, that is not even true because Seraphine is often not here, spiritually. She goes on her after-dinner journeys to the astral plane. I watch her, those delicate eyes rolled back, in ecstasy or pain I don't know, and I wonder if she is not gone for years, aeons, seconds. I still feel nothing, and I have given up trying, but I stay close to protect her. What would happen if some earthly event affected the physical body while the spirit is on the astral plane? Would she instantly come back, tethered as she is by the silver thread? Or would the silver thread be severed? Perhaps it would be bliss for her, but torture for me. She insists on being close to death at all times. Can you answer me these questions, Carl?

When she returns to herself at the table, less than an hour has passed for us skeptic mortals, yet she has the bewildered look of someone who has been away for some considerable time. And she seems rejuvenated, as if each time she grows a little younger. And semi-translucent in the half-light, part of her still in another dimension. It is almost like she has reset time when she comes back, rewound a ticking clock. Time has reversed its flow for her. Would that it be the other way round, since I am the one so much older!

No, the only constants are myself and the house. The words of Leadbeter about tulpas and thought-forms resonate. Did I create it in my mind? Tulpas are supposed to be beings, living things, not inanimate objects. But this house, I hesitate to describe as an inanimate object. It does seem alive—like it knows things. It has a strange fluidity to it, as if it has grown out of the ground organically, no doubt the effect of the mirrors that twist and bend the light. And that infernal black mirror on the opposing cliff that seems to warn us, shame us, showing us a shadow version of ourselves.

Tulpas are conjured by thought, and it is remarkable how much the house corresponds to the image I had in my mind of the perfect house. It was the fairytale castle that I dreamed of as a child. Perhaps my version of that which all little girls dream of. I dreamed it night after night in my childhood bed, fleshed out the details, engendered it, and now it has manifested into something real. Without a concession or a compromise anywhere, I achieved every impossible whim and feat of dream architecture. Perhaps that gift of unlimited wealth, combined with the genius of Cécile Butticaz… Well, you see what women achieve without the hindrances of men?

Only the weekly arrival of the newspapers from Paris reminds me of the dates. The world continues to come to us, and yet Seraphine and I have not left this mountain in…years. My God. I have tried to discuss these questions of time with Seraphine, and she professes to understand and agree, but is remarkably serene about it all. Does she possess some higher spiritual knowledge? Or does she always seem to know the right thing to say?

"What I have learned, my love," she said, "is that time does not exist. Our perception of time is the only thing that separates us from seeing the interconnectedness of the world when planes of time are equal. When the past is the present is the future, and everything that exists is part of each other, duration delivers nothing but ghosts. One moment is every moment combined. We can remember the future but only imagine the past." She says that true understanding comes from stepping outside of linear time to experience the eternal.

These are the sorts of things Pauline and Nathalie and I would witter about to each other after a long night of smoking opium, but we would be as platitudinous as Seraphine is profound. She has some otherworldly understanding that I cannot grasp.

Our heads have no doubt been turned by the men of science

who have frequented here. And women of science too, I should say—we have had Marie Curie, Isabelle Stone, Madeleine Pelletier, of course... Science is changing at a terrifying pace, and yet it is remarkable, Carl, the points of convergence that are appearing between science and spiritualism, even as they would seem to be poles apart. The new thinking, as I'm sure you know, is that time and space themselves are not at all what we thought.

Do you know of this Planck constant? Of Einstein's special relativity? So many of our fundamental beliefs about the universe may be an illusion. It is heartbreaking, is it not, that everything may be an illusion. I don't want to believe it. We had a chap here the other week who claims that time is not real. And he is not one of those crackpot spiritualists, nor does he romanticize the idea like Seraphine; he is a Cambridge professor of physics with a scientific explanation for it. He said that the past, present, and future are all just shards of the same, all connected. But how could our tiny minds comprehend that? And why does the future not then reach back into the past to make everything perfect?

I feel that there are things we are not yet meant to know. We are trying to prise open a Pandora's box of knowledge for which we are not ready. And something will come along to stop us.

By the way, the dress code has always been very liberal here, to put it mildly—some of our guests wear barely anything at all —but everyone seems to be moving towards whites. Kumara has infected us all with his eerie simplicity. Seraphine wears only white linens now. Of course, she looks divine—like a candle, her billowing hair the flame, her sleeves and skirts the dripping wax. You will be relieved to know, Carl, that I am still doggedly wearing my breeches, cravats, silk waistcoats, and riding boots. Although I am starting to feel like a stranger in my own home.

Yours affectionately,
Lydia

CHAPTER 7

Cyrus

2035

The next morning, Haydn met him at the bottom of his staircase and escorted him to the Physics Department on the bus. She attempted to take his arm as they crossed the road, but he shook her off: "Yes, yes, don't fuss. I'm blind, not crippled." But he said it kindly, and the truth was that he did need her. He couldn't get around anymore, and it was time to admit his limitations.

It felt good to be sitting with her on the bus, heading on an intellectual adventure. He watched the blurred city career by through steamed windows, and they sat in amicable if slightly nervous silence. He didn't want the journey to end. If only they could stay in this limbo forever. Screens suspended from the bus ceiling had rolling news, which he could not see, but not a single passenger was watching either—they all looked away. In a waking sleep.

Public safety announcements were interspersed with news items. He could see only the colors of the screen background, but the audio came over the bus tannoy in its calm voice: "Tran-

103

sition to war phase... What to do in the event of a siren... Always be five minutes from a shelter... Get your emergency kit in order..." Such efforts were being made to prepare for the worst-case scenario; it was as if they were manifesting it. Conjuring a war into existence like one of Leadbeter's thought-forms. There was an air of unreality to the whole thing, a fine line between the horror and the absurdity.

The Physics Department was a blend of architecture ranging from the eighteenth century to the postmodern, mirroring the evolution of physics from Newtonian to quantum. They entered the reception, Haydn scanned her retina, and signed Cyrus in as a guest. He was more nervous than was reasonable. He felt as if he were going into a hospital, about to receive some potentially terrible diagnosis. She led him through a maze of corridors that joined buildings together, and he squinted at signs to take in words and phrases that he would never understand, that the vast majority of the human race could never comprehend. Spintronics and Magneto-Transport Lab; Neutrino Oscillation Detection Group; Nonlinear Dynamics Dept; Ion Beam Research Group.

He peered into various rooms as they continued, wondering at the mysteries that unfolded within. He thought it odd that nobody seemed to acknowledge Haydn—it was such a small department, surely there would be hellos, some nodding and smiling? But then, to his dismay, Roy Lightman emerged from a seminar room, unmistakable in a white lab coat, white shirt, and cream-colored jeans. Cyrus's heart sank as Roy blocked their path.

"Ah, hello, Haydn. I see you've booked Optics 3. Faffing about with mirrors again, are we?"

So, he did know her now. Some flicker of unease and possibility made Cyrus shiver. Lightman had sabotaged him before; was he capable of such a hoax? At a time like this?

"And this is a perturbation in an otherwise stable system—a philosopher in the physics department. What on earth are you doing here, Cyrus?" Yet somehow, Roy didn't sound surprised. Cyrus had a strange sense that his whole appearance was rehearsed.

"Oh, same as young Haydn. Faffing about with mirrors. She's going to show me a little experiment that arose from our class discussion."

Roy theatrically moved to one side and held out his arm for them to pass. "Don't go breaking any of my equipment, old man," he called after them.

Optics Lab 3 was a small, dark room in the oldest part of the department, a Victorian building whose interiors had seen better days, with yellowing walls, cracked tiles, and wainscotting, choked with dust. Less of a laboratory, more of a museum. The Victorian sash windows were blacked out so that the room was devoid of natural light. The walls were also painted black, and the lighting was dimmed. A rectangular wooden table sat in the middle of the room, and the walls were lined with workbenches cluttered with obsolete instruments, future antiques. Tarnished brash and cloudy glass fought for space with plastic meters, instruments too commonplace to be collected or even stored. Cyrus felt his way along a workbench, feeling the instruments. A vintage lens fell at his touch, and the glass shattered.

"Sorry."

"It's fine," said Haydn as she swept the pieces into her hand. "No one is going to report that missing."

Haydn noticed Cyrus's expression and said, "Not very fancy,

is it? Classical optics is not really the thing anymore. It's all about quantum photonics and spectroscopy now. But it does mean that it was easy to book a room."

"For faffing about with mirrors?"

"Exactly."

Haydn placed Cyrus close to the table in the center of the room, and again, he appreciated her subtle management of his poor sight. Her hands on his shoulders as she maneuvered him felt warm and alien, so infrequently did he touch another human. She moved around the table to face him and explained the setup. On the old table, which bore the traces and stains of decades, centuries of experiments, was a standing mirror to his left, oval-shaped, a simple looking glass. And opposite the mirror, to his right, around fifty centimetres away from it, was a toy house that stood on top of a tissue box. The toy was a lurid pink and blue plastic thing, a branded princess palace, a caricature of the mansion from Lydia's letters.

"I've tried to recreate the two sides of the gorge." She patted the top of the mirror, more animated than he had ever seen her. "Here we have the fault mirror, made of obsidian, which is an igneous rock. Obsidian was one of the earliest materials to be used as a mirror, thousands of years ago. At its smoothest, it reflects light as well as glass does. Sudden seismic events like the earthquake that would have created this fault mirror can cause clean breaks in the rock. So, imagine this to be the smooth obsidian cliff that Lydia described. That you…that Daphne saw. And here," she tapped the toy house, "is Lydia's castle on the other side. Sorry, it's a bit silly. It's all I could find. If you look in the mirror, you can see its reflection."

"And I am standing on the bridge," he said.

Just like Daphne did. Like we both did.

"Exactly. This is the only accessible viewpoint even now. Don't forget that the bridge wasn't there in Lydia's time. It was only completed after the war. So, in 1915, there was an earthquake in the Vuache mountain range; La Mandallaz mountain lies at the end of this range, and the Mandallaz mountain split. Part of it fell away—the part on which the chateau stood. It was little reported since everyone was so preoccupied with the war, but we know from seismic records, and from damage further down the Vuache fault, that there was a significant tectonic shift, and the Vuache plate split and dropped." She placed her palms together, then dropped one abruptly. "We don't know exactly who was at the house at the time, but it was when Lydia was away during the war.

"So we can imagine that the cliff on which Lydia's house had been built suddenly split from the mountain and dropped, taking the house down with it." She removed the tissue box and placed the house down on the table, emphasising its vertical movement down. The mountain split, and what was revealed behind was another fault mirror. "That's the smooth cliff that you saw—where Daphne saw the house."

"Okay," he said. "So now the house lies on a ledge halfway down the cliff, with another fault mirror behind it."

"Exactly." She placed another mirror, identical to the first, just behind the house. Immediately, they were dazzled by a complex kaleidoscope of geometry. The house was repeated countless times in both mirrors, in parallel lines tracing back to infinity. He leaned forward to see it better.

"An infinity mirror is created. Beautiful, and terrifying. Imagine what the inhabitants of the house would have felt, would have seen."

"If they survived the earthquake."

"If they survived the earthquake." She nodded. "But it's more complex than that. We need to bring some more mirrors into the equation. Because the cliffs had other patches of obsidian, not just the large mirrors but other, smaller mirrors on each side. We can only make an estimate as to their position, but when we add them at exactly the right places, something else happens."

Haydn took two smaller standing mirrors and placed them on either side of the first mirror, on chalk markings that she had prepared. But she held her hands over them. "Imagine that this cliff, the first fault mirror, opposing the house, has a couple of other sections of smooth obsidian. Look what happens now. Ta-da." She removed her hands from the mirrors with a flourish, and the house disappeared.

Cyrus moved a step to his left, then a step to his right. No house. He leaned in closer and peered—had his sight suddenly taken a turn for the worse? No house. Finally, he put his hand in front of one of the small mirrors…and the house reappeared. He waited for her explanation. She was clearly enjoying a dramatic pause.

He felt inexplicably tired.

"It's an invisibility cloak," she announced. "Basically, when you have mirrors placed in a certain way, you can effectively hide an object. It's sometimes called a Rochester cloak because it was developed at the University of Rochester. They have a big photonics department. But what's amazing about the invisibility cloak is that it just uses standard mirrors, nothing fancy. So, we've had the materials to become invisible for thousands of years, just staring us in the face."

It was the first time he had seen her smile.

"An optical illusion," he said, more petulantly than he had

meant to. "People have been creating illusions with mirrors for centuries."

She wasn't deflated. "Yes, but this is different. It was spontaneous, unplanned. Not created by humans intentionally, but a freak of nature. Nature made the house disappear."

They were silent for a while. Haydn moved the small mirrors a couple of times, tentatively, making the castle flash on and off. Like a switch. "You see the fragility of the setup—the mirrors must be in exactly the right place."

Eventually, he spoke. "You're saying the house was there all along, it was just hidden by natural mirrors in the rock. Like a blind spot. So why could Daphne see it and I couldn't?"

Haydn held up her finger and moved to the door where there was a dimmer switch for the ceiling lights. As she dimmed the lights, the castle appeared. She brightened and dimmed them repeatedly, playing with the image of the castle so it flashed like a zoetrope, flashed until he could hardly bear it. He thought of the zoetrope in Lydia's letters. "Imagine this light is the sun," she had said.

Haydn moved to the window and opened the blinds, just a small amount. "Keep looking."

As a ray of sunlight entered the room, the chateau flickered into view. She opened the blind a little more, and it disappeared again.

"There are certain angles, very precise angles, and levels of light, at which the cloak fails. If you gave me a week, I could write some equations for it. It's surprising how reliable the cloak is if the mirrors are in the right positions. It is very difficult to create the right light conditions and angles for the house to reappear. The mirrors, combined with the position of the sun, act as a kill switch."

"So, Daphne may have been in the right position at just the right time of day when she went back by herself?"

"Exactly."

"But she said she had seen the house when she was a child. What are the chances it would happen twice?"

Haydn's face fell. "It's possible. It's also possible that she had never been to the house. She remembered it another way."

"What do you mean?"

"We'll get to that."

A gaggle of students bustled past the door in the corridor outside, and then their voices suddenly hushed at the sound of a siren. Cyrus and Haydn's hands both automatically went to the iodine kits around their necks, as they waited—*here it comes, here it comes, it's happening*—but the sound was only a police car or ambulance somewhere in the distance.

Cyrus took a deep breath. "A house hidden in a permanent blind spot. What would that have meant for its inhabitants?"

"They most likely died in the earthquake."

"I saw the cliff. There was no way on or off it, even in 1980. So, 120 years ago, even if they didn't die, they would have been trapped. And in the middle of the war, with the world preoccupied…"

Cyrus tried to imagine the earthquake. He didn't know why it made him tearful. At the same time, as convinced as he was that they were fake, he felt strangely invested in Lydia's letters. He felt moved by her love, her energy, and by the strange, ethereal Seraphine and the hazy life they were building for themselves. A house that felt at once in another world and yet profoundly connected to everything in this one. He had been willing them to make it, but these women couldn't seem to keep the world out.

They stood in silence for a while. What were they doing? Mourning a group of people who may or may not have existed, who may or may not have died in a castle that may or may not have existed.

"You've shown me some trick mirrors, Haydn. And no doubt it's a very impressive physics project. But when you came to my rooms in First Week, you said something about the house being in superposition. That's not the same thing at all. If I understand correctly…" He could hardly bear to bring it up, so suddenly tired did he feel. "Superposition, in the quantum physics sense, means the ability of a system to be in multiple states until it is measured. Like Schrodinger's cat—both alive and dead until we open the box."

"Yes. That's it. That's the other thing, Professor. About the physics."

He wished there was somewhere to sit down. Instead of standing opposite this girl, mirrors and toy houses between them, as she bombarded him with theories in a field he could not comprehend.

"It isn't just a visual cloak," she said. "It's a *temporal* cloak."

"Well, yes, in the sense that you don't see the house during the time when it is actually there. You're hiding the house in time."

"No, it's more than that. Have you heard of the quantum Zeno effect?"

"Well, the Zeno effect I've been teaching for forty years." Cyrus often mentioned Zeno's paradoxes in his tutorials. The ancient Greek philosopher had several paradoxes, and the paradox of motion, or the arrow paradox, had regularly come up in his Disappearing House problem. "*You can never get there.* In the arrow paradox, Zeno stated that, for motion to occur, an object must change the position that it occupies. If you take the example of an arrow in flight, Zeno stated that at any one instant of time, the arrow is neither moving to where it is, nor to where it is not. Therefore, it can never really go anywhere. But the quantum Zeno effect… I'm not sure… I suppose I'll know it when you tell me."

Haydn nodded. "So. The quantum Zeno effect allows time's evolution to be slowed down. A system cannot change while you are observing it. That's a paradox of quantum mechanics. Hence, Zeno's arrow, which doesn't seem to move. At the precise moment you look at it, it appears still. So, if you measure—and by measure I mean observe—something frequently enough, you can effectively slow down the time evolution of that system. The more observations you make, the more you can slow down time. Usually, we are talking about fractions of a second."

"And if you have an infinity mirror, you have…"

"Infinite observations." They both said it at the same time. "The house looks at itself for eternity." She nodded.

"But…forgive me, Haydn, I'm a layman…I thought that quantum effects like superposition only applied to quantum objects. Things only behave like that at the microscopic level."

"Not always. The principle is that non-quantum objects cannot be in superposition because the waveform collapses due to the object interfering with its environment. But this object, the house, does *not* interfere with its environment, because it has disappeared. It cannot be observed from the outside. There-fore, the principles of quantum mechanics apply."

His brain was spinning. "According to the letters, Lydia filled the hall with mirrors. Wouldn't that affect this… Rochester cloak?"

"It's impossible for me to recreate that, so I can only approximate and abstract."

"Ah, the little falsehoods that grease the wheels of science." But Cyrus knew he was the last person to criticise abstraction. "So, what does it mean if one can slow down time infinitely?" he asked, knowing it was a rhetorical question. "What would be happening in that house?"

"I don't know. That's why I need you, Professor. Cyrus. It's a question for philosophy as much as for physics. It's more than hiding things in time. It's hiding time in time."

"It could mean that no time passes at all. It could still be 1915 there."

"Perhaps. Or another time, completely. We don't know how time passes between those mirrors. The extent of the time dilation. It's like a point outside of time. Or all times at once. A different dimension."

An Archimedean point, he thought. *A point outside of time.*

"If Daphne found the house," said Haydn, "she could be living there now."

Cyrus's heart lurched at the intrusion of it. "Just…as she was in 1980?"

He picked up the little toy house, turned it over and over in his hands, and felt the grooves in the plastic. "Schrodinger's House," he said. "Both there and not there."

"Yes, exactly."

Cyrus set the toy down. "If I understand correctly, in Schrodinger's cat example, the cat is both alive and dead. The waveform represents the two possibilities for the cat—alive or dead. The act of opening the box, looking at the cats, collapses the waveform into one of the possible outcomes, and we look at a reality. Is that correct?"

"Yes, exactly."

"But what would be the possibilities for the house? Because there are more than two, destroyed or intact, its inhabitants alive or dead… Are there infinite possibilities? And if Daphne did find the house, looked at it, did the waveform collapse in 1980? What state did it fall into?"

"At this point, Professor, these are questions that I don't think physics can answer. I mean, I can make up a bunch of equations. But as you know, physics nowadays is believing whatever you want to believe, then finding the equations to prove it. That's why I need you. I think this is a question for philosophy."

Cyrus's head was spinning. "What question? Define your question, Haydn." He tapped on the table with an urgency that surprised him. "Is it 'What would happen if time stopped?'"

"My question is: 'Should we look at the house?'"

Fifty years of his teaching had all distilled down to this absurd question: *Should we look at an invisible house?* Absurd, and yet he had a strange feeling that the stakes had never been higher. What would happen to this Schrodinger's house if they looked at it?

"I still don't understand why you need me, though. It feels as if you are torturing an old man, dredging up the past."

"Because the questions I am asking can't be answered by physics, only by philosophy. We cannot calculate the probabilities of different possibilities for the house—whether it was destroyed in the earthquake, whether it was trapped in time, whether Seraphine was trapped in the astral plane, and so on. I think we must make a moral judgment. Should we look? Should we disturb the universe?"

It was too much. The thought of Daphne, still being twenty-five years old. Trapped in time. Or maybe not trapped. Perhaps eighty years old, like him, or a corpse. The thought of a house trapped between dimensions, a house that defies space and time. That obeys the new laws of new physics, where anything is possible if you can only imagine it and make an equation. He gave in and smiled. Haydn did not.

"I know this is a game," he ventured. "What I don't know is why."

They left the Optics Lab and walked out of the Physics Department in silence. Haydn helped him down the steps wordlessly. There was still an ease to their being together, despite the new tension. They stood face to face on the pavement. Out in the blinding sunlight, where passers-by were going about their day as if there was no nuclear war on the horizon, as if he had not just received such a revelation. Was it a revelation? The world certainly felt different, but how?

"I'm not sure where to go from here," he said. "I need to think a little. A lot. And I feel there are things you are not telling me."

"Could you consider the possibility that I am being earnest? We have mirrors out there in the Hubble Space Telescope"—she gestured vaguely into the sky—"that can take photos of the beginning of the universe. Mirrors already show us the secrets of time. Is it so hard to believe that mirrors could manipulate time?"

He sighed, looked around him at the blur of colors and traffic and bodies, and looked around him for an answer. "I may be going blind, but I'm not going mad."

I am.

"What is it you want from me, Daphne? I mean, Haydn." His heart skipped a beat at his mistake, but she didn't react.

"I want you to tell me whether we should look at the house. Not as a philosophical exercise. I mean, for real. I want to go to the French-Swiss border and look at the house."

"How can we look at something invisible?"

"Professor. What a question. It sounds like one of your assignments."

"I'm serious."

Haydn said, "I thought of using a drone. Trying to climb up or down is too dangerous. And I believe there must be some sort of security—military or otherwise, preventing access."

"Why do you say that?"

"For the same reason I say that Lydia has been wiped from history. Someone wants to stop us from finding the house."

Us. Why does she keep saying us? "In that case, a drone would also be dangerous. I'm sure it's prohibited."

"Worth a try though."

Cyrus sighed. "No one is supposed to travel, Haydn. And how are you going to get to Switzerland? Presumably, you used up your annual flight allowance to arrive here."

"Yes. But I still have one travel credit, and we can take the train. There's a philosophy conference at the University of Geneva next month. I thought I could go as your amanuensis, so we can both get a travel visa."

"We. I see. You have thought this through. Haydn. One travel credit. How will you get back?"

She didn't answer. Again, he had a sense that they were coming to the end of all things, and there was nothing but darkness ahead. Nothing to lose, perhaps.

Dear Carl,

I am sorry to report that things have rather gotten away from me since I last wrote. Seraphine is well. We are as happy as ever. But…the Chateau des Miroirs has taken on a life of its own that we seem powerless to control. Sometimes I feel that I have conjured up a house that doesn't belong to me. I summoned it from some other part of the universe where it already existed. Am I afraid of it? The house does seem to have a slightly malevolent presence. Or, perhaps not the house itself, but the shadow house in the fault mirror. It knows things. I shiver when I look at the shadow house in the mirror, the black mirror that shows us the darkness within.

Our soirées continue—call them salons or séances, I suppose—but Seraphine has made this place an outpost of theosophy, and she continues to access the astral plane so that she has one foot in this world and one in another. I have tried to access it too—Lord knows I have tried—but I cannot feel it. My sensual pleasures are rooted on the earth. Instead, I watch her as she goes, her eyes closed, eyelashes fluttering, head rolled back, and eyeballs racing behind the lids. She always has Kumara to her right—I'll come to him in a moment—and me to her left. We hold hands, and I hope that some of their electricity will flow into me.

Instead, I remain her guardian here on earth at the mirrored table, and I imagine her attached to me by the unbreakable silver thread between this world and the next. When you love someone, you must let them fly, and they will always come back. I am quite content to be bound by mortal sight when I have Seraphine and this perfect landscape to look at. There are parts of her that I can never know, and why should I?

But Seraphine is much changed. I cannot tell if she is serene or troubled, even as those two states of mind would appear to be very different. She appears to have gained some other-worldly knowledge that has profoundly affected her and that she cannot share with me. I don't feel that she is lying to me, but rather that she is protecting me. It's very odd. I always felt that I was the wise one, the provider, and the impulsive one—yet now she is all these things. Because at the same time that she is imbued with a mysterious sadness, she is determined to live every moment as if it is her last. She says yes to everything, laughs more, dances more, all in the service of her mantra: "There is no time, there is only now. And we must seize our happiness here."

And now to this Kumara, or Krishnamurti, or… He has many names. Mouthpiece of the World Spirit, Lord of the Akashic Records, Keeper of Time, and so on. He simply never left. Nobody ever asked my opinion on the matter. Leadbeter appears to have "given" him to us as a gift, and I suppose it is a great honor. I can't help feeling it is nonsense—it's no different from the Christian idea of the Second Coming… I don't really know what Seraphine thinks about this, but she seems to like having him around, as a sort of validation. And she has been more than tolerant of my friends, so I suppose I will make an effort. But the whole thing makes me uncomfortable. Particu-larly as this Kumara is not the innocent lamb that Leadbeter makes him out to be. I know for a fact that he has spent nights with Pauline and Nathalie. And while there's nothing wrong with that, he is here for more than sex and spirituality.

Far from being an uneducated village boy, he has a degree in civil engineering from the University of Bombay, and he has designs on this place that are completely at odds with our vision. Yesterday, there was a team of men here with charts and spirit levels, surveying and goodness knows what else, and they are planning all manner of unnecessary things—a bridge across the gorge, a hydroelectric dam, power lines… If this is the march of progress, I don't want it. We never wanted a bridge.

Their aim seems to be to overcome elemental obstacles; to harness nature, rather than adapt to it as Cécile did. I feel as if I have accidentally declared war on this mountain valley, and now I am powerless to stop it. Events move on relentlessly, and my heaven is rapidly becoming a hellscape. Seraphine can no longer go down to bathe in the river, for the valley is filled with machines and predatory men. Dynamite, for goodness' sake. Now when I stand on the edge of the cliff and look into the vast mirror, I see not a Manet but a Hieronymus Bosch painting. Workers bore and hammer and blast, and the cliffs are scarred by scaffolding, the birdsong drowned by the calls of men.

The peace I created here was an illusion. Perhaps man is destined never to be satisfied. There must always be a yearning for more, more. Perhaps we cannot choose the path of romance without also choosing the path of ruin. I know I have said this before, but nothing great has ever been achieved without the motivation of either love or will to power. I know what I find most beautiful, and I know what motivated me. I also know what motivates men. I feel so naïve, letting these men into our fortress of women. Especially as that is how men want us to be —naïve.

The specter of hubris now haunts me as I regret not building a simple chalet. Seraphine wanted nothing more. We must always overreach ourselves. Just because I can build a castle doesn't mean I should. Perhaps in temptation is encapsulated the whole of human history. Just because you can doesn't mean you should. I know you have warned me before about my impulsive nature, and here is the consequence.

Who are these people in my house? These men who have invaded our fortress of women? It seems the specter of war is upon us as well. Talk around the dinner table is increasingly of war, or rather, the relentless peace talks that only ever seem to bring war closer. I receive all the newspapers here, and although the rise of Germany is alarming, there is a militaristic tone all over Europe. Some dangerous fools are even saying that war is needed, as a cure for the decadence and boredom that has become the rot of society. These interminable peace conferences are just buying time while each power builds up its forces. They talk of "peace" when they mean "war"—it is pure semantics and hypocrisy.

When I read L'Illustré now, amidst the fashion photography and reviews of the latest theater plays, there are mentions of armies and new types of guns—the tone is different. We are drifting towards something terrible, inexorably. Seraphine still believes in peace, and I admire her goodness, but I fear that goodness will not be enough. I admire Seraphine's pacifism, but I fear it is naïve, as naïve as I have been.

Perhaps you are better informed on this than I, Carl, out there in the real world. And the theosophists who frequent our little unofficial center of theosophy profess to have inside knowledge on this from the "spirit world," which infuriates me. I don't need a spiritualist to tell me war is coming. And it is not due to dark forces warring in the Astral Plane. Leadbeter goes on about Atlantis and Atlantean times, and the coming war as part of a great cosmic battle. He talks about the "Lords of the Dark Face of Atlantis" as if it is a proper thing, and everyone nods knowingly. What dangerous rot.

This is what he said during his last visit, or words to this effect: "We are all trying, so far as may be, to prepare for the coming of the Great Teacher. Realize that this great War is part of the world-preparation, and that, however terrible it may be, there is yet the other side—the enormous good that is being done to individuals. Perhaps in the distant future when we come to look back upon it all with greater knowledge and with wider purview, we shall see that the good has outweighed all the frightful evil, and that though the old order changeth, giving place to new, it is only that God may fulfil Himself in many ways."

Of course, this is all entirely at odds with the supposed atheism of theosophy. Who is this God? Some monstrous wave of Nature declaring war on Man? Nonsense. It is Man who has declared war on Nature. And Nature may take its revenge.

These engineers that Kumara has brought here seem to be entangling war with spiritualism as well. We had Rawson and Forhan here, two spiritualist engineers—goodness knows who invited them—and they talk of "thought power" and "psychic offensives." Last week, Seraphine hosted the French Society of Savantes, and a certain Monsieur Bardonnet detailed plans to identify German foreign policy through clairvoyance. Sometimes I feel I am caught in a nest of very stupid vipers.

It is the height of irresponsibility to claim that the coming war is a clash of good and evil. There is no good and evil. There are no secret societies. There are men and machines. But worryingly, they may have a point. Let me explain. As I told you, the Steiners are close confidantes of Moltke and his elite generals. They regularly go over to Germany to give them spiritual advice. And the Steiners have told us that not only General Moltke, but the Kaiser himself, is deeply influenced by the occult. According to Steiner, Moltke views a war as "a necessity anchored in world evolution" so that "Germany can fulfil its cultural mission."

Moltke believes in the imminent Second Coming of Christ and an apocalyptic battle between German and Slav, the outcome of which would determine the next stage in world history. He apparently talks of "the atmosphere charged with a monstrous electrical tension…" that demands to be discharged.

"Absolute hogwash," I told Steiner. "Do you realize how irresponsible it is to entertain these ideas? History is decided by a few idiot individuals—do you really want one of them to be him?"

This paradigm of cosmic struggle, a battle against materialism, Germany's destiny, world cycles, rebirth. Irrational beliefs like these, with notions of war as redeemer and deliverer—these notions have always been our downfall.

And so it seems that Steiner's esoteric teaching has had a concrete effect on the events of his time. These men are filled with delusional ideas about chiromancy and the evil eye. And they somehow manage to tack these ideas onto new technologies. Alchemy becomes poison gas; the Great Wheel becomes a great tank. If they are making battle plans based on tarot cards and crystal balls, then what hope is there for any of us?

As I predicted, Seraphine has let the manicured gardens grow wild, and I must confess the flower meadow is glorious. The chateau is almost floating in a sea of flowers. There are poppies everywhere—they grow marvelously well in this climate—and so, of course, there are plenty of jokes. About opium, of course, but also about Persephone. We are all literary types after all, and Swinburne's "Garden of Proserpine" feels unnervingly suitable. With Seraphine as the queen of the underworld. Guests jokingly warn each other not to pick the poppies, or they will go into a waking sleep and forget why they came here. Seraphine loves to pick them. She says they symbolize the transience of life and the approach of death. She says it with romance rather than horror.

Your affectionate friend,
Lydia

CHAPTER 8

Cyrus

2035

After he parted with Haydn outside the Physics Department, Cyrus realized it was going to be a monumental task to get back to college alone. He cursed himself for being too proud to use his cane. At some point in his life, he was finally going to have to swallow his pride. Autumn was in full flow now, leaves swirling and the scent of rust and damp. These rusted days had been taking on new meaning every year as he got older, and now they meant something else again. The certitude of the seasons was both a comfort and a terror. Nature's calm acceptance of, and preparation for, the inevitable. It was mirrored in their preparation, their acceptance, and there was horror in that. Because while winter and summer changed little, an incremental warming each year, every time war came around, it was unpredictable. And worse.

Journeys on foot were no longer times for reflection; his focus had to be on staying safe and upright. But even after he finally arrived at the college, exhausted, he was unable to clarify his thoughts or focus on anything for the rest of the day. He was deeply unsettled, and he imagined that had been Haydn's intention. He reeled from one emotion to the other; mostly anger that this girl had had the audacity to suggest his wife might still be alive. And with that, all the old feelings of guilt and shame and grief and confusion and disbelief came flooding back.

Cyrus spent the afternoon half-heartedly learning about the quantum Zeno effect, obsidian mirrors, and Reynolds cloaks, hating himself as he did it. Mirrors he could grasp; the concepts, the diagrams, even the equations. Mirrors, with all their mystery, were something the human brain could attempt to process. But anything quantum was a different matter. Quantum ideas had always both fascinated and terrified him. Despite his intellect, he was unable to fully grasp quantum mechanics on anything more than a superficial, rote-learning level. He simply could not picture it.

It was as if humans had accidentally discovered something they weren't meant to know, something from another dimension. Desperate snatching at technologies just beyond their reach: this was the Promethean gap that had led to every war. A waveform collapse—what did it mean? He could describe it in words, repeating verbatim what he had read, understanding the language. But could he really visualize it? Something that existed as a multitude of ephemeral possibilities suddenly collapsing into one thing. His inability to picture quantum ideas in his mind left him with aphantasia, and that was terrifying, because soon, his mind's eye would be all he had left.

He was not going to countenance magic mirrors and disappearing houses. He who had devoted his career to the concept of a Disappearing House. He preferred the idea that the letters were fraudulent. But how to go about proving it?

Putting aside questions of magic and fantasy, Haydn's essay had presented Cyrus with an interesting philosophical conundrum. How to prove that someone didn't exist? He had never considered this angle and could see no way around it. A negative proof of a negative. It could be a fascinating topic for a dissertation, or even a paper of his own. And it had been a long time since he had considered the possibility of writing a paper, so he had to give Haydn that at least. She had piqued his interest in something, if not the subject at hand.

Proving or disproving existence was a central tenet of philosophy. Reality, God, consciousness, the soul. He had taught Bertrand Russell's teapot many times as a core part of the syllabus. The teapot analogy was about the burden of proof. If Russell were to claim that there were a tiny celestial teapot orbiting the sun somewhere between Earth and Mars, too small to be detected, it would not be reasonable for him to expect others to believe him, just because they cannot disprove its existence. The burden of proof would be on him, Russell. Belief without evidence is irrational. So, in this case, the burden of proof would be on Haydn to prove that Lydia didn't exist. For him to disprove the existence of Lydia, it would be like disproving the existence of God, with Haydn as the fervent Christian believer, telling him that:

I cannot prove that Lydia exists, so you prove that she doesn't.

If you can't, then Lydia exists.

But this was the opposite. This was the teapot reversed, with the burden of proof on him to prove that Lydia didn't exist.

I cannot prove that Lydia doesn't exist, so you prove that she does.

If you can't, then Lydia doesn't exist.

Except this was complicated further by Haydn's claim that someone had actively wiped Lydia's existence. Any potential proof had been removed. Cyrus could not prove that Lydia had been actively erased simply by not finding any evidence of her, and that was the point. He would have to catch "them" in the act—spot a mistake and find a chink in the armor. And who this mysterious "them" could be was another question entirely. It was possibly the most fascinating philosophical problem that had ever been presented to him. There was that, at least.

At High Table that evening, he took advantage of a lull in the conversation. Opposite him sat Dr. Diego Cortez, a young economic history lecturer who taught the Statistics for History undergraduate course.

"I have a question for you, Diego. It's a historiographical question, I suppose. Let's say you wanted to erase someone from history. How would you go about it?"

"Oh, fascinating question." Diego nodded with enthusiasm as he hurried to swallow his food. "It depends on what you mean by erase. And what the purpose is. History is written by historians, and so many people and events have been forgotten just by not writing about them. It's called Memory-Holing. They just fade away naturally."

"Let's say it was more formal than that. A complete wiping of someone's existence from all records." Cyrus tried to keep his voice nonchalant, curious. He hated that his blindness made both he and whoever he was speaking to raise their voices. The whole table was already listening, and Diego was addressing the room.

"Aha, well. That would be complicated to achieve. History is a tapestry, and people's lives are tapestries, interwoven with others. With a monumental effort, you could destroy all records directly connected to a person. But that doesn't account for others' records, secondary records—for example, they might crop up in a photo, or a diary. Everybody touches someone in some way."

Cyrus prodded. "I imagine it would be more difficult in the modern era. Since there is so much information out there."

Diego thought for a moment. "Actually, I think it is probably easier nowadays. The haystack is bigger, but the needles are easier to find. Most of us have been 'born digital.' How often do we print out photos of ourselves? Write letters by hand? I can't remember the last time I did either of those things. There is far more information out there in the world, but it's all digital, and therefore searchable. Someone born in the Information Age can exist online only, with hardly any physical records. And most literature nowadays is 'gray literature'—never existing in print. It's the physical records that are harder to destroy, and so I would argue that someone from the past—at least the recorded past, and certainly the nineteenth and twentieth centuries, when most people became literate, and societal records became more organized—would be harder to erase."

Cyrus said, "There's something rather sad about that. The idea that we only exist digitally, I mean."

"Yes, indeed. Particularly in view of what might be about to happen. Who knows what technologies will survive."

"There's also something sad about the notion of erasing someone from history. I'd like to think that, as you said, everyone makes a difference to someone."

"Damnatio Memorae," Professor Tanner exclaimed, putting down his wine glass, wiping his white beard on his napkin, and expanding his chest as if he were about to begin a lecture. He

communicated by way of the occasional grandiloquent statement that didn't invite a response. "Condemnation of Memory. It's a very Orwellian thing, but in fact we've been doing it for thousands of years. Emperor Nero, the pharaoh Akhenaten, Trotsky, the purges of the Chinese Cultural Revolution, the Romanovs, Aristide in Haiti…"

"And yet we have heard of all these people…" pointed out Cyrus.

"That's the thing, it's extraordinarily difficult to do." Diego nodded. "And you often end up making martyrs of the 'victims'—iconoclastic vandalism, for example, when you go knocking down statues—you only end up drawing attention to the person you're dishonoring. You end up being an agent of memory rather than the opposite."

"There was a time when we talked of 'cancelling' people, do you remember?" said Cyrus. "In the days of social media. A very judgmental era. The problem is they often ended up being talked about more."

"Of course, we say all this, but who knows what *has* been successfully wiped from history? The unknown unknowns. Who will be uncovered at a later date?" Diego was in his element now. "I think there's a distinction we can make between *damnatio memoriae*, which is the condemnation of a deceased person, and *abolition memoriae*, which refers to the actual erasure of a person from historical texts. The former is more about shame, to guarantee only negative memories. That is easier to do and is the essence of propaganda. It's just an extension of historiography. The latter is rather more sinister. Definitely Orwellian. The 'memory holes' of 1984 were intentionally complete and undetectable. Who knows how many future regimes Orwell inspired to actually do it?"

Roy Lightman weighed in. "I should think all regimes have memory holes, even the good ones. What was it Hilaire Belloc said during the First World War? 'It is sometimes necessary to lie damnably in the interests of the nation.'"

"Belloc was a fairly awful person, if I remember my World War One history correctly," Cyrus interjected. "Turned out to be terribly antisemitic."

"Oh yes indeed, but he wasn't wrong in this case," said Roy, leaning over to allow the server to refill his wine glass. "It isn't safe for people to know everything. Ideas will have their time. Knowledge will have its time."

Their discussion had generated interest, and Professor Mary Moyo, the Mistress of the College, interjected from the head of the table.

"You're asking the wrong person, Cyrus. Those who control the past also control the present, and quite possibly the future. So, you should be asking the person who controls the past. The keeper of memories." She smiled and nodded towards the woman sitting to her left, the only other woman at the table. Kathryn Gardner, college archivist.

Kathryn had been at the college since before computers had been installed; matriculating in 1993, she had seen the whole Information Age from its inception. Somehow, she had managed to weather every storm—digitization, human resources upheavals, AI, pandemics, war. She was the still point of the turning world, steering her ship of books expertly. Now in her seventies, she was irreplaceable, dogged, calm, severe. Cyrus was embarrassed that he hadn't asked her, but more embarrassed that he couldn't remember the last time they had exchanged words, even though they had sat at the same table night after night for years.

"You're at risk of being erased from history yourself, Cyrus, since you haven't let me near your papers." Kathryn spoke in her deadpan schoolmistress manner, raising laughter across the table.

It was an old joke, and almost the only thing she and Cyrus had between them now. Kathryn had tried and eventually given up trying to persuade Cyrus to properly organize his Disappearing House files. It was a source of tension between them that had eventually become a gulf. He had a nagging sense there was another tension between them as well, but he wasn't sure exactly what it was, and he preferred not to think about it.

"I always think it's the cruellest thing, to be erased from history," she said. Her crystal, singsong voice sounded strange, one of the voices not often heard around the table. "Surely all we want is to make our mark. What a shame, for nobody to remember you."

"Shame is the word," nodded Diego. "You're exactly right that it's to do with shame. *Damnatio Memoriae* was about erasing people considered dishonorable."

What dishonorable thing had Lydia done? Women and minorities had always been erased from history simply by omission. Was it as simple as that? Nobody had thought to write about her? Her existence erased simply by the unconscious act of forgetting? Just as Cyrus had erased Kathryn's existence from his radar, simply by not thinking about her. In his world, she had barely existed, even as she dwelt only a hundred meters away from him all these years. He brushed off the thought and went back to Lydia. Or was there something more sinister at work in Lydia's case? *Her absence proves her existence.* He thought of Haydn's essay. If Lydia were real, what could she have done to warrant such shame, such forgetting?

As the others traded anecdotes about Roman generals, cancel culture, and the legality behind the Right To Be Forgotten, Cyrus looked at Kathryn again, as if for the very first time. With his failing sight, his memory of her blended with the blurred vision in his pupils. She looked her age, not the sort of woman to make concessions to standard notions of beauty. But she was still pretty.

Her hair was silver now instead of blonde, but it was sleek and combed into a neat half pony-tail, not unkempt like his. From this distance, he couldn't make out the rest of her features, and he imagined that he was just imprinting his memories onto her face. Kathryn Gardner had still been a graduate student when he had joined the college as a Junior Lecturer. Ancient and Modern History, if he remembered correctly.

And she had been pretty even then—considered a catch. He had a vision of her at a college ball in 1999. The Commemoration Ball, perhaps. He seemed to remember her standing on the steps of the quad, wearing a red satin ball gown. Or was that his memory getting mixed up with Lydia's letters? Seraphine's red dress, Seraphine on the stairs of the Folies Bergère. Images conflated in his mind.

Somehow, like him, Kathryn had never left. She'd entered the college library like a cloister and never came out. Fifty years of curating. Fifty years of memory keeping.

"What are you up to anyway, Cyrus?" asked Diego, stirring him from his reverie. "This sounds intriguing."

"Oh, just a thought experiment. It came up in a logic problem. An ontological proof…"

Which wasn't entirely untrue. It was a logic problem—how to prove the non-existence of a person, versus how to prove the existence of a person has been wiped. He had always had an uncanny ability to distil everything in his life down to a philosophical conundrum. Perhaps it was the only way to live, to place oneself at a point outside of things. To watch oneself as if in a mirror.

Dear Carl,

Seraphine and I had our first serious disagreement yesterday. The war is tearing us apart before it is even upon us. If only it were as easy as finding your soulmate. That's only the beginning. We have to continue dealing with the rest of the world. After the assassination of the Archduke, it was only a matter of time before things spiraled. Poor Seraphine, with her dreams of pacifism… What will you do, Carl? Will you have to join up? These poor young men. Please do not be one of them. I pray that you are already too old to enlist.

Liane's son is dead already, his plane shot down in one of the first battles. She is broken. When I think of everything she sacrificed for him, only to have his life snuffed out in a moment. I rode my horse to Avenières yesterday, too anxious to wait for the mail to be delivered. There was a line of young men in the square, standing in the pouring rain, and a large wooden sign that said, *"On les aura!"*—"We'll get them!" As if they are going off to some drunken brawl. Every able-bodied male is enlisting. Every doorway had a woman, and every face was the same—a grim mixture of terror and resignation.

I galloped home with the newspapers. The house was still asleep, but Seraphine was in the garden collecting blackberries. She was such a picture of innocence in her white linen dress, straw hat, and with her basket. I took her to the steps so we could talk privately. The house is full of ears.

"My dear, we must make plans. War is here whether we like it or not. We cannot just wish it away."

She paled. "But surely we can be safe here? Switzerland is neutral."

"Nothing is neutral, Seraphine. Apart from anything else, the French border is just over there. And there are German spies everywhere. For a start, we cannot have Steiner and his friends here anymore. We do not just put ourselves at risk."

"But he is already here, and he is our friend."

"Yes, he is our friend, and he may not mean any harm. But nothing, it seems, is safe from German spies. He and his wife are in with General Moltke. And yes, yes, it's mostly about tarot cards and ghosts, but if one of our Parisian guests here should slip up and reveal something, no matter how small, about French strategy… And there's a telegraph position only a few miles from here, which invites trouble."

"We can help. This place can be a sanctuary, a farm… Everything will unfold as it should." Seraphine seemed so calm and knowing about this. As if she knows some profound political aspect that I have not understood. But it is only her naïveté talking, and I told her so. I was too harsh and I regret it: "You cannot be so naïve, my child."

"Do not call me your child."

"I know you cannot bear it, but you must. We all have to do our part now."

But when she said something to the effect of "Perhaps all the world's artists can hide here until the war is over," I got angry with her, for the first time.

"There may not be fighting here, but there may be battlefields of a different kind."

"Yes, of course," she said. "Spiritual battlefields."

"No, for goodness' sake, you silly girl." I almost shook her.

And then I apologized, for it is not her fault she is so good, so unworldly. And they are so very convincing, these theosophists. It is my fault. Seraphine brought in her trade unionists and socialists, while I was more interested in dancers and poets and fortune tellers. Perhaps I have been the one living in a fantasy land, not her. Both of us playing, pronouncing on how to make a better world. And all the while, the blade of history had been sharpening around us. We look at ourselves in the fault mirror, and we see exactly what we are. Then we carry on regardless. Is there anything more soulless?

The construction works have been abandoned now, since all the young men are gone. The bridge had begun on both sides, so it looks as if the middle has plummeted into the abyss. It might as well have. The gorge is like a deep, vast grave. The cliff is a wreck of broken staircases and loose ropes—I see its ugly reflection in the fault mirror. The mirror shows me what we have become. So here it is—the wreckage of progress. I knew, I knew all along, and yet I did nothing.

That evening, we dined by candlelight. Another interminable party, this juggernaut of meaningless, determined fun that I don't seem able to stop, with an array of sparkling guests from Paris, Zurich, and Vienna. The only difference from our usual evenings is that my two serving boys from the Avenières village, Robert and Marcel, have gone to war. Only seventeen and eighteen. So, we served ourselves, and I was sickened that we found it a novelty. I looked around the table and wondered —some of these people could be Deuxième Bureau, or Abwehrdienst—how would we know? We have done nothing but play. I turned the World's Fair into a doll house filled with toys, while out there, the dynamos have been developed for destruction. There are worse crimes than vulgarity, yes—complacency.

For the first time in months, war was noticeable in its

absence from the conversation. Instead, talk was of Strauss and his new opera, *Ariadne auf Naxos*. I do not blame a composer for composing at a time like this—why should he be a politician? But I do blame us for having more interest in music than in the end of the world. Eventually, my nerves got the better of me and I slammed down my glass so hard that it shattered, wine spilling over my hand like fresh blood.

"Lydia, whatever is the matter?" said Seraphine, jumping up to wipe the table with napkins.

"The matter is that we are sitting here guffawing about dissonance in Strauss as if nothing is happening out there. This interminable repartee." Perhaps a little hypocritical of me, in hindsight, given that it was I who created this fairyland and who has embraced it more than anybody else.

"But what would you have us do, Lydia?" asked someone—I can't remember who.

And the whole table turned to me for answers. Lydia always has the answers, usually by throwing money at a problem. I muttered something about the end of US isolationism and our moral duties, but what do I know, for I am rich, frivolous, and uninformed?

The air was thick with confused desires that night. I left the party and went out to the garden to sit on the stone steps at the edge of the abyss. Lights and shadows from the house reflected in the fault mirror. Seraphine slid next to me in silence.

"We can't do nothing. We can't hide," I said. "We must do something. I won't have this place commandeered as some tele-graph center. If it were only more accessible, it could have been a military hospital. If only. We have all sleepwalked into a nightmare."

She put her head on my shoulder, and everything was fine between us again, but there is a rift now. Perhaps I have created her as much as I have the house. Nathalie once said to me that I had manifested my idea of Seraphine just like one of those thought-forms. She said that when you're in love, you never really know whether your elation comes from the qualities of the one you love, or if it attributes them to her; whether the light which surrounds her like a halo comes from you, from your own heart, or from the meeting of your sparks. At the time, I was indignant, but now I understand a little.

However, my love remains as strong as it ever was. We love the whole person, flaws and all. God knows I have my monstrous flaws, both physical and mental, yet she accepts and embraces them all. I picked up a rusted piece of chain, left over from the abandoned windlass.

"We think ourselves chainless, and yet we do not have free will any more than we have souls."

"I think we have both," she said. You can never truly know another person, even your twin soul. She has some serenity that comes from a higher knowledge that I don't possess.

"If the chateau is commandeered by the war," I said, "I should like it to be a hospice or place for refugees, or a farm or a school. Not some command station for spies and whispers and telegraphs."

I was preparing to tell her I was going to leave, and she seemed to anticipate it.

Seraphine said, "We have land and animals. You see how good I am at growing things. You have made me strong. I will provide for people."

"I have squandered my wealth, but I will not squander my

abilities, Seraphine. Marie Curie is setting up an ambulance service, X-ray machines, and all. I am a good driver—there are very few of us women who can drive. And the men are needed for…other things. I lived in France long enough to join the Expeditionary Force."

She was silent. We faced the void, the same as we had done that first day when we sat in my Daimler on the rue Faubourg. Back then, we had all the time in the world, and now it seems we are coming to the end of time. There was dancing in the fault mirror, reflected from the house. We heard shrieks of laughter. Someone playing Satie's "Je Te Veux" on the piano. The last days. I see them dancing in the black obsidian, and they have no idea that this may be the end of all things.

"If you don't want me to go, I won't. I'll stay here with you."

"No, you should go. If there's even a chance you can help, you should. Just come back to me, Lydia, if you can. Or if today is to be our last day, I want it to be like this. Not in darkness or pain. Just together, in the moment."

Seraphine allows me to go. If she had begged me to stay, I would have, but she wishes for me what I wish for her—the fulfilment of our potential for goodness.

"I will protect you," she said, her green eyes glassy with tears. I don't know what she means—is she going to protect me via the astral plane? But she seemed so sure.

"When you come back, we will make this place good. Perhaps we can fill it with children."

"Children, yes. Women and children."

And why not? Who knows what we will be when this is over?

When we looked up at the stars that night, there were new lights in the sky. The spattering glow of Howitzers on the horizon and the swipe of search lights, their crossing streams striping the dark. The blade of history is sharpening, and we will write the next chapter in blood. Pray for me, Carl, and I will pray for you. Even if we don't believe.

Your affectionate friend,
Lydia

CHAPTER 9

Cyrus

2035

The next morning, after his teaching was finished, Cyrus wandered over to the archives, half-formulating plans to request some innocuous document or other that had nothing to do with *damnatio morae* or Lydia Temple or disappearing houses. The College Archive was a crypt underneath the main library, accessed by outdoor descending stone steps without any railings. Adrift, Cyrus cursed his failing eyes as he inched his feet towards the edge of each step, praying that nobody would see him from the quadrangle as he struggled and rush over to help. Finally, at the bottom, he almost fell against the door with relief. This could not go on. He knocked and entered.

"We open at two," Kathryn said in a cheerful yet forbidding singsong, without looking up. "Unless you make an appoint—oh, hello, Cyrus." She peered at him over her glasses.

He tried to conflate the blurred image of the room with his memories. He hadn't been here for years. He had pictured the Archive as some dusty antique shop, a curious miscellany, an accumulation of second-rate treasures that hadn't quite made it into the library's main display. But it was more complex than that, a whimsical combination of vintage and modern.

Kathryn sat at a desk, behind which was the vaulted crypt filled with the whirring college servers, their lights twinkling like frantic miniature warnings. Kathryn's office area was more like the chaotic antiques shop that Cyrus remembered. There was some semblance of order around her computer on the huge oak desk, but the rest of the room was piled with artefacts. An eighteenth-century globe in aged wood, a huge pile of scrolls in one corner, open folders of ornithological etchings and architectural drawings. One sideboard displayed brass optical instruments like those he had seen in the Physics Lab. And every inch of wall space hung with portraits. The also-rans of the college's history who hadn't made it onto the walls of the Great Hall.

She sat back in her chair, relaxing her pose and looking around with him. "Yes, I am a bit of a magpie. Some of these things are deemed not important enough to display, but I can't quite bear to put them in storage. Things left by students over the years and decades and centuries. There's a story in every one of them."

She got up and walked around to his side of the desk, where she picked up a red-and-gold Venetian mask. "These things, for example. Paraphernalia from a vacated student's room." She put it in his hands, for him to touch, and he had a horrible vision of the future, when people would have to do this for him every day. He felt the velour contours, the gold braiding, the eye holes, and the elongated nose. And he felt her smooth, cold hands as she passed it to him and then took it away gently.

Katherine continued. "It's very old—the student probably

bought it in a charity or antiques shop. Who wore it before? How many parties over the decades and centuries? How did the student's night unfold—was it for a ball? At this college? Did they meet the love of their life that night? These are questions I could answer in so many ways, from forensics to fantasy. And this."

She picked up a bright red shiny box, a twentieth-century standard-issue office money box. "I had to get a locksmith to open it. Nothing special about it from the outside. But inside, all these scribbled notes." She rummaged through scraps of paper—faded yellow Post-it notes and sheets torn from lined notebooks. He could just make out scrawls of biro.

"Do you remember our college days," she asked, smiling, "before mobile phones, when we just had to leave notes on each other's doors or in pigeonholes in the Porter's Lodge? And just hoped we would eventually find each other? Those were the days."

"Yes, those were indeed the days."

She looked at him for too long. Some tug of memory nagged at him, something to do with Post-it notes, and he couldn't tell if he should explore it or bury it further.

"Anyway, these are scrawled exclamation marks, hearts, scribbled meet-up instructions, inside jokes—it's almost hiero-glyphics. And it appears utterly mundane. But if it's so trivial, why did someone lock it in a safe? I like to think there's a story."

"Yes, interpreting that could be...quite something. I could give you all sorts of philosophies about objects having their own existence, even consciousness. Panpsychism, object-oriented ontology..."

"Oh, I'm sure you could, Cyrus." She laughed, putting the

box down. "But I'm not a philosopher, just a romantic. Why not romanticize an object, elevate its power?"

Cyrus said, "Why not indeed. All objects are artifacts—they store memory, so they all have meaning."

"I used to think that when I retired, I might write the stories of my favorite objects, even if I have to invent them."

"That's an excellent idea," he said. "And when will you retire?"

"I think we are all retiring soon, don't you?"

After putting the artefact on the table, she turned to face him and folded her arms. He could smell the waft of a perfume that gave him a lurch of nostalgia, sent him somewhere. She wore a pale yellow cashmere sweater, green tartan skirt, and brown leather boots. From this distance, he could see the cross around her neck, a rather austere gilded pewter thing, gothic-looking, too young for her, as if left over from her student days.

"That's a very Catholic-looking cross. Are you religious?"

"Oh no. This is another of my salvaged treasures. I like to wonder who wore it before. I was, once. Catholic, I mean. But I lost my faith a long time ago. If there is a God, I imagine he's a vindictive little man. What about you?"

"Oh, same. I went on a pilgrimage once. The Way of St. James. Didn't end well."

There was a silence, not fully unpleasant.

"It's difficult not to become a hoarder in my job," she mused. "Because everything tells a story, even the most mundane object. Everything is connected to someone. But of course, part of my job is to select what we will remember and what we will forget. I get to consign things to the dustbin of history."

"What power you have." He smiled.

"What can I do for you, Cyrus?" It seemed to come from far away. So much seemed to come to him from far away now, as he retreated into his mind, involuntarily or voluntarily, he wasn't sure.

"Ah, yes. You remember that discussion last night about *damnatio memoriae* and so on?"

"Indeed."

"I wanted to ask you some more about it."

"Really? Last night, you seemed more interested in what Diego and Martin had to say."

He fumbled for a reply. He wished she weren't standing so close. He didn't know where to look.

"I'm teasing you, Cyrus. I long ago gave up trying to get a word in edgeways at that table. Go on." He stumbled against the empty chair between him and the desk. These were unfamiliar surroundings, and he felt suddenly vulnerable.

"Here, why don't you sit down?" She helped him into the chair, as effortlessly as Haydn in her acknowledgement of his failing sight, his age.

He settled into his blurred surroundings. He had filed Kathryn away in his mind as some bespectacled woodland creature, beavering away amongst fading box-cards. Now he remembered that it wasn't quite like that. She had an infectious energy.

"It's not how I remember it, this place."

"Well, you haven't been down here for a long time, Cyrus."

"You don't suffer from the lack of natural light?"

"I'm not down here all the time. And…well. Soon we may all have to get used to a lack of natural light."

"That's a lot of paper on the desk. What are you working on? It looks like you're bookbinding."

"I am! It's strange—archival science has come full circle. I spent about twenty years digitizing everything, and now we are re-physicalizing everything. Because we don't know what kind of technology will be available to us after… Well, it's wonderful to be able to use my book-binding training again. It's a labor of love, creating these books, these beautiful things. We are the keepers of memory, and soon it may be that memories are all we have."

"Indeed."

"So. *Damnatio memoriae.* If I understand correctly, you want to find out if it is possible to erase someone from history."

"Not exactly. It's a little more complicated than that. I want to consider how to prove that someone had been, you know, erased from history. It's a conundrum. A hypothetical. But let's say it had been done—putting the reasons to one side—how would you go about proving it? I thought I might approach it from another angle…with your help. What if I approached the question like this: instead of asking, 'Is it even possible?' let us assume that it is possible, and that it has been done. How can I prove that it has?"

"Interesting. It's a tautology. If the person doesn't appear to exist, then either the 'cleansers' of history have done their job, or this person never existed in the first place. Either way, the evidence, or lack of evidence, is the same. It's like saying unicorns don't exist because nobody has ever seen one. No, that's not the right metaphor. It's like trying to prove the existence of God. If God were hiding from us. Perhaps you could prove that it has been done by catching the cleaners in the act. Finding evidence of their cleansing activity. Digitally, that's very unlikely. If they have the capability to erase someone, they have the capability to cover their tracks. So, what if they made a mistake? If something slipped through the cracks?"

"Exactly! How would I go about doing that, do you think?" He suddenly felt an energy he hadn't felt in a long time. She was playing along, and it was…fun, almost.

She laughed. "But who are these cleansers we are talking about? This is all intriguing, Cyrus. Are you going to tell me who this erased person is?"

"Oh, it's purely theoretical. It's from a problem of philosophy. Something a student brought to me."

"Don't give me that. You always did think I was born yesterday."

There it was again, beneath the playfulness, some flicker of a hint that his memories did not align with hers; something had happened in the past that he had chosen to forget. Some flicker of some feeling just beyond his grasp, that perhaps he didn't want to grasp. He would have to give her some more information. Would that be so bad? Was it somehow betraying Haydn?

"Alright, well, there is a rather interesting story behind it, as a matter of fact."

"Take me to lunch, and I'll allow you to tell me all about it." He saw a flash in her face of the girl she used to be. Had he never noticed, or had he just forgotten, that she had a rare and beautiful smile? "And I don't mean in the dining hall. I'm fed up of sitting in silence with my tray, eavesdropping on students. Let's go out. Stranger things have happened. Gardner's on the High Street has a very nice lunch deal."

She put on her coat and gloves and took his arm, not as if he were blind but in another way. He saw another glimpse of something, the corner of a curtain lifted on another life that could have been.

Gardner's was noisy, the lunchtime rush a clatter of clinks and mingled conversations. The restaurant was decorated in the Art Nouveau style, all glass and metal, too many mirrors, not enough soft furnishings. Rushing waiters wore traditional black and white. It was at the upper price-end of the city's eating establishments, so there were few students, mostly senior academics and professionals.

"The acoustics are dreadful in here, sorry," said Kathryn as they took a table in the window.

"It's quite alright. I may be blind, but my hearing is excellent." He preferred the noise. It helped to dilute what they would talk about, minimize the importance of it.

They ordered house salads and made some small talk about the weather, the war, until he could avoid the topic at hand no longer. He told her about Haydn, the letters, and her essay. He felt the unease of betrayal. Haydn had not given him explicit permission to tell anyone. But then, she had not asked him not to tell anyone. She wanted him to believe by any means necessary, and it was a release to share. However, he stopped short of telling Kathryn about the Optics Lab, the superposition, the mirrors. Was it too far-fetched? He wasn't ready to vocalize thoughts he hadn't yet processed.

"What a story," said Kathryn, when he'd finished Lydia's tale. "But what I don't understand is, *why* does Haydn claim that this woman has been actively erased from history? For what reason? What did this Lydia do?"

"She hasn't explained that."

"There's rather a lot she hasn't explained. Why on earth

would we believe her? Surely, it's just a way of justifying the letters—the letters that she wrote—and a rather poor one."

"That was my first thought. But it would have been easy for Haydn to insert some false clues if she really wanted to convince me. Put a few things about Lydia Temple on the internet."

"True."

"Let's indulge the notion that the letters are real. So, we must explain what happened to Lydia Temple in the annals of history. Let's say you wanted to erase someone from the college records—all trace of one person's existence. How would you go about it?"

Kathryn thought for a moment. "From the college records? I could do it. It's hardly the Akashic records down there—our archive is large but finite. I'd start with the digital records— easier to search. Then I'd go through the physical records. The difficulty would be covering my tracks. Patterns of systemic removal, tampered physical records, unusual record requests, or ban notices… But if this were done systematically, then the perpetrator would have covered their tracks. Yes, I could do it. I might have to forge a few documents in place of the ones I destroyed. Printed photographs would be the most difficult. You can't easily replicate those.

"But that's just a college record. I couldn't control the rest of the world. Let's say, for the sake of argument, I had the means to remove someone on a global scale, digitally. I still wouldn't be able to control all the physical records. The secondary sources. Mentions in derivative texts.

"If Lydia was who she said she was, she touched so many people's lives. And we have the advantage of the pre-digital era, the possibility of physical evidence. There must be something they missed. The mysterious *they*.

"We can't prove beyond a reasonable doubt that Lydia didn't exist. Search exhaustion wouldn't prove anything, particularly if someone had gone to the trouble to wipe her. Instead, we need to prove that someone tried to erase her by catching them in the act. Missing or altered records, gaps in records, incomplete historical accounts, contradictory accounts."

"But that might imply travel." He hadn't been further than London in years, and international travel had become almost insurmountably difficult. Haydn's plan for them to go to Geneva was surely impossible.

"Not necessarily," she said, picking at her salad. "Physical records are more likely to have been destroyed in the areas local to where she lived. Travel could be fruitless. We need to be creative."

"Haydn already found a few examples. Unexplained gaps in the personal histories of Natalie Clifford Barney, Rudolph Steiner."

"A few examples aren't enough to prove anything. I'm intrigued, Cyrus. I love a good mystery. I will help you. But I need something to go on, for these secondary sources. Can I see the letters? There must be some clues in the letters, some suggestions that might lead us somewhere."

For the first time, Cyrus realized that he had not made copies of the letters. He had made some notes, but he had no physical evidence that the letters existed at all. What had he been thinking?

"I gave them back to Haydn. I'm not quite sure why I didn't make copies. I suppose these days I am relying more and more on memory."

"A dangerous thing to do."

"Indeed, especially for us elders."

"Speak for yourself, Cyrus," she teased. "I'm seventy-five, and I may look it, but I don't feel it."

"You don't look it. You look…very good." Was that the best he had? He had never been good at this, and decades of no practice didn't help.

"Thank you, Cyrus." She laughed. "I'm sure you can barely see me."

"Anyway, I can give you some names, some references. Things I remember from the letters." He felt stupid, unconvincing. But she didn't flinch, instead taking out her notebook and pen with enthusiasm. "Go on. Give me a list of the people she mentioned."

"Haydn will have searched those references already. If she had any proof, she would have told me."

"Haydn must be nineteen. I have been doing this for fifty years."

Cyrus looked out of the window, going back over the letters, the words imprinted on his mind. "Lydia claimed to be a member of the Amazons—the women of the Parisian demi-monde. She was a close friend of the writers Natalie Clifford Barney and Pauline Tarn. They frequented the Folies Bergère and the Moulin Rouge together, and the women visited Lydia's chateau on several occasions."

"Ah, then I must check the annals of La Fronde. You know, the French feminist newspaper. It was published daily in the 1900s—surely, she would be mentioned."

"Then there's the theosophy connection. Rudolph Steiner and Charles Leadbeter were supposedly regular visitors to the chateau. It became an unofficial headquarters for Swiss theosophy. And the engineer Cécile Butticaz was apparently the architect of the chateau. There were also vague mentions of Debussy, Marie Curie. But who knows if Lydia was just a name-dropper? It's like a Who's Who in those letters."

"I must say, it's all very exciting."

"Even if we find evidence, it still doesn't answer the question of why."

Their coffees arrived, and the bill, which Cyrus took clumsily. Kathryn smiled her thanks.

"May I ask you something?" he said, to break the silence. "If I remember correctly, you received a double first, a scholarship, and a Mackintosh prize. How did you end up being a college archivist for almost fifty years?" he asked. Somewhere in his mind, it had been designed as a compliment, but he instantly regretted the choice of words and the sentiment. He felt her energy drop. No wonder he had been single since Daphne.

"Well. What a lot to disentangle there." She sat back in her chair and looked out of the window. "Firstly, you do remember correctly, and unnervingly so, about my scholarship and prizes. As for 'ending up' being a college archivist, I think you know the answer to that. In the 1990s, this university was still a boys' club."

"Our college still is."

"You say that with a certain amount of amused pride, but I think it's rather shameful that we only have two women at High Table. Anyway, I was blackballed from every postgraduate job for which I applied."

"Surely not."

She shrugged. "Perhaps not actively, but implicitly. At that time, nobody wanted to hire women in their mid-twenties. Risk of maternity leave and all that. So, I got a temporary position as Assistant Archivist, and I found that I loved it. While you say 'almost fifty years' as some sort of failure, I see it as a success. I love my job, and I'm proud of it."

He was ashamed, but there was a sparkle in her eye. She was teasing him. Confronted with his academic snobbery, he could not deny it. There was, after all, a huge amount of prestige to be had in being the keeper of memories.

"I've published more than you, Cyrus." She said it without an ounce of arrogance, still teasing him. "In fact, I've published more than most of the dons in this college. Perhaps not in the most important journals, but in the small world of archival science, I feel I can hold my own."

The following silence seemed to say a lot, but he couldn't decode it.

"Marie Vance," he said suddenly.

"What?"

"Marie Vance. That was the alias that Lydia used when she became an ambulance driver in the war. She had to pretend to be French to enlist. Maybe we could try searching for Marie Vance."

"There. A good lead. I'm going to enjoy working on this."

"Thank you. I'm sure I'll remember something else…"

"Well. You know where I am."

The lunchtime rush was over now as they headed out onto the High Street. She put a gloved hand through his looped right elbow, as he marked a rhythm with his cane in his left, and they walked in step effortlessly. The rain clouds had cleared, and the sun had burst into a glorious autumn afternoon, with the smell of petrichor and the burnished leaves, the heartbreaking march of time, the genius of nature. It no longer felt like just one more season of man.

"I had a very nice lunch with you, Kathryn," ventured Cyrus. "Thank you. And what a beautiful day. I find this to be the finest time of year in Oxford."

"I find one only has to decide that a day will be perfect for it to be so. But yes, I also had a very nice lunch, thank you. We should have done this long ago. Now, in return for my help, you must let me come and help with your files, Cyrus. It's intolerable. One fire and it's all gone forever."

"How do you know I haven't digitized them myself, Kathryn?"

"Have you?"

"No."

"Well then."

Dear Carl,

It is hard to imagine how this letter could possibly reach you, given the circumstances. Between the confiscations, redactions, miscommunications, and mistakes, it is hard to believe any letters get through at all. But I shall send it anyway, as I send almost daily letters to Seraphine. I have not heard from Seraphine since I was at Amiens, although that is understandable. This is such an outpost. It feels like I have found myself at the last place on earth, at the end of the world. And it is indeed hell.

I write to you from Souham Barracks, Evacuation Hospital Number One. This is the address to use if you wish to try and write to me, although who knows whether it will still exist next week. You must use my alias, Marie Vance, since I am obliged to pretend to be French. I hope the Americans will join the war—since we have abandoned our peaceful isolation policy, we might as well come and assist—but until then, I have been perfecting my French accent. I am sure my colleagues and superiors suspect, and if this letter is intercepted, they will find out. But I doubt anyone would begrudge my being here. I knew my cavalier road skills would come in useful one day, and I have no doubt I am the fastest ambulance driver in this war.

We are currently around five miles from the front lines, and my main occupation is to drive an ambulance between the casualty clearing stations and the hospital. I also help to load the bodies and perform what changing of dressings and application of antiseptic that I can. Occasionally, the fighting comes so close that I drive through artillery fire, and I am currently wearing an eye patch due to a nasty bit of shrapnel. If I lose the other eye, I don't know what they will do with me.

At night, I share a dormitory with the other nurses, around twenty of us. It is a far cry from anything I am used to, and when I lie shivering under a rough blanket, no pillow, I dream of Seraphine in our satin sheets, and velvet coverlet, and sumptuous cushions. I try to manifest it like one of Leadbeter's thought-forms. In any case, we sleep little. Between the cries of suffering men, the hissing of bombs, the whining of planes, and artillery fire in the distance, there would be little opportunity even if we were not on duty every four hours.

The hospital is such a vision of chaos as can only be surpassed by the battlefield, and I have seen both. I have held down a screaming boy as his legs are sawn off; I have been thrown to the floor by an officer gone mad, having lost his whole regiment, who then dashed his brains against the wall. The worst was that he survived.

Some nights and early mornings, I am called to the front line, and I drive through an eerie yellow-green fog. Other nights, the skies are brutally clear, the stars over the battlefield tormenting us with unreachable heaven. The exploding shells like some evil parody of stars.

I always lived for sensation, seeking it out wherever I could. Well, be careful what you wish for. My senses have come under attack in ways I could never have imagined. Deafening roars, foul stenches, thin and rotting food, miserable textures, and sights that cannot be unseen. I have seen death so often that it is not strange or fearful to me.

It breaks my heart when the young men in their beds dictate letters for me to write to their families. Such bravery and selflessness, their only concern being not to upset their wives and mothers. What breaks my heart even more is when I see fresh troops marching towards the front, filled with jokey bravado. These young men were sold enlistment as some boys' adventure. They are little more than cannon fodder.

What have we done, Carl? Is this what the World's Fair has led to? I remember with bitterness the men's dinner table talk at the chateau about humanizing war—that monstrous contradiction. Earnest debates about when to allow certain types of artillery, mines, poison gas. The conduct of war so much more interesting than its prevention. Nothing could be further from humane than this.

Or am I wrong, and this is what humanity truly is? Our shadow selves, out of control. Is this what the black mirror was showing me? Sometimes, I understand what the theosophists mean when they talk such nonsense about Atlantis and Good and Evil. For there is certainly evil here. I don't see how we will ever recover. For the only way to win a modern war is to kill so many of the opposing side that they cannot carry on. And therefore, the bigger the weapons, the bigger the killing machines, the better. Where will it end?

Well, no doubt this letter will be redacted down to nonsense or not sent at all.

Do you remember, Carl, when I wrote to you about that moment of first love, when I kissed Seraphine for the first time, and I felt it to be an archetype? That we were all the lovers that had ever been and ever will be, feeling the shared electricity of that first kiss? Driving through the battlefield was the polar opposite. I have experienced the archetypal moments of horror and despair.

The other day, a Zeppelin crashed less than five hundred

meters from the hospital. It came soaring in like some giant white creature, some angel falling from the sky, blocking out the sun, yet we could hear the screams. It exploded the moment it touched the ground, and now all that remains is a tangled mass of wire trellis and charred bodies. Three survived, so now we have these German prisoners, their burns covered in bandages.

I have received no news from my other friends, which again is no surprise. Most of them don't even know where I am. But I have heard that life continues in Paris almost as normal—salons and Strauss and the Moulin Rouge. It is hard to fathom how that could be possible, only a train journey away from this hellscape. I wonder if people have any idea what this war is really like. In our minds, we are still stuck in Franco-Prussian times, with swords and bayonets and pistol duels, feathered helmets and brass buttons and breeches, genteel battles followed by genteel balls. You could send your husband or son off to war, and he had as good a chance as any of returning, a decorated hero.

But there are no heroes in this war. And the greatest villains of them all are the generals sending these boys out to slaughter each other. Same battle tactics, different weapons, weapons that can kill a whole generation in no time at all. Man's ingenuity wasted on this obsession with destruction. I am again struck by this notion of the Promethean gap and how we are destined to misuse our gifts. Our morality lags behind our technology.

Your affectionate friend,
Lydia

CHAPTER 10

Cyrus

2035

There had been a change in the world that day Haydn had first come to him with the letters. Nothing tangible, but a new energy. And now that Kathryn had appeared in the picture, everything had changed again. He couldn't define it, didn't feel inclined to think about it too much, but it felt good. The march of time had changed pace, but whether it was racing or slowing, he wasn't sure. They had no more meetings or lunches, although he often found himself looking across the quadrangle from his rooms towards the library, wondering if perhaps he should… Preparing the words he might say…

He did telephone her a few times as he remembered pieces of information from the letters that might be useful to Kathryn's research. Seraphine's purchases of antiques in 1901—Lydia had mentioned a specific shop. The order of the mirror from Venice and its transport to Avenières. The address of the de Valleirys on Rue Faubourg, the names of Marie Vance's various barracks during the war. He looked forward to dinners at High Table now, whereas before he had been bored in advance. They didn't discuss Lydia at dinner; something unspoken between them kept. But he felt a new comfort and acceptance in her presence.

He saw Haydn at their weekly tutorials, but she behaved as if nothing had happened; minimal contribution to discussions, adequate essays produced, straight out of the door at the end of the sessions without making eye contact. He couldn't tell if she was deliberately avoiding him or giving him space. Occasionally, he saw her red hair around the college, like a cursor, a laser. He could see her when he could barely see anything else, as if she had that colored hair especially for him and his failing sight. A beacon, to guide him, to remind him. He felt he should try to get to know her. But he also wanted to keep her at arm's length, this curiously one-dimensional, single-minded being. If she turned out to be a fraud, if none of this was real, then the journey would be over, and he was rather enjoying his new sense of purpose.

It was late November, the eighth week, almost the end of term. The trees were nearly bare, their leaves forming vast piles of debris on pavements and corners. On the gloomiest days, there was barely any light at all. The world preparing for darkness. There were muted preparations for Christmas.

His phone rang one morning. "Cyrus? It's Kathryn. I have some results for you. I'm not sure my search has been exhaustive, but for the sake of the archives, I need to get back to my regular work. I've been neglecting it. So what about if I come over and share?"

"Did you find anything?" His voice choked as he asked.

"Well. Not much. But perhaps that's the interesting part. Anyway, I'm coming over, ok?"

It was strange and good to have her in his rooms. She

looked around with curiosity, peering at book spines, trinkets, and he hoped there was not too much dust, wishing he had tidied up. He had inadvertently left the door to his bedroom open, and she glanced in at his lonely single bed, carefully made.

"What a lot of mirrors, Cyrus. If I didn't know you better, I'd think you were extremely vain."

"Ah, yes. I'm not sure when I started collecting mirrors, but I rather like the effects of the reflections. It makes the room look different every time I take it in. And it certainly confuses the students that come for tutorials."

"Yes, it must be quite unnerving. You are cruel."

"It's not that so much as… It makes them think differently. Does something to their brains, to have all these competing perspectives."

"We all see what we want to see in the mirror. Occasionally, the truth catches us unaware, a flash from another dimension, and we recoil in horror. Well. Have you lived here this whole time? Fifty years, isn't it?"

"Indeed. You have been here even longer, though."

"Yes, but I have moved around. I would have loved to live in college, but that's reserved for the proper dons like you. Anyway. I have a little flat off the High Street. When I bought it, there was nothing special about it, but now it turns out I'm almost on top of a bunker entrance. Prime real estate. So, I'm the person to know. When the time comes."

She was about to sit down. "Actually, can I pull up this chair alongside you? It will be easier. No, no, don't get up."

She shuffled the heavy chair around to his side of the desk, and they sat side by side. She took from her bag a blue ring-bound folder on which she had written "The Letters Project" in font so large it must have been for his benefit. "I was going to write 'Lydia Temple' or 'The Lydia Temple Letters', but something stopped me. Do you ever get the feeling you are being watched? Probably just me. Adding a little adventure to my life.

"First things first." She placed the binder in front of him and patted it with both hands, but left them there to keep it closed, still possessing it. "At face value—I mean, based on a superficial amount of research—Lydia Temple did *not* exist. There's nothing. Not just the official records, but the incidental, secondary ones too. No mention in the diaries of prolific writers who were supposedly her close friends. Not a single mention of anyone resembling her even in La Fronde. All those feminist friends of her, and she was not mentioned once in the female-run newspaper of Paris. With her apparent love of scandal, not a single mention in the gossip columns of the time. No purchase of land, no building of a house, no psychiatric hospital stay pre-1900. All those people whose lives she apparently touched, and they didn't mention her at all.

"But that's where it gets interesting." She smiled sidelong at him, shuffled closer and began leafing through the pages. He breathed in her perfume and felt the gossamer touch of her cardigan as her arm brushed against his.

"There are some gaps that don't make logical sense. Pauline Tarn was a prolific diarist. She wrote diligently every day. Except for a few notable and unexplained gaps—could they have been the times she was with Lydia?"

Cyrus said, "Lydia did say that her chateau was a sort of secret club that nobody talked about."

"Well, either that or they did talk about it, but someone else removed the offending references. And on a more general level, as you pointed out, if someone wanted you to believe she had existed, it would have been easy to insert her name into a couple of academic papers online. Add a description of her to a couple of websites. But if someone wanted you to believe she had never existed, they would have to hope that you didn't find this."

Kathryn held up a finger in triumph, then leaned over and took another plastic folder out of her bag, from which she carefully removed a print-out of a photo—a very old, black-and-white daguerreotype-style photo. He squinted at the image, but it was a blur until she described it to him. A young woman, sidelong to the camera, crouching down to meet the eyes of a child, both smiling. Standing next to the crouching woman was another woman, dressed in men's clothes, looking proudly at the camera, striking a pose with a cane. And behind them, the Ferris wheel of the Great Exhibition in Paris. In the background were groups of people strolling in Edwardian clothes, the towers of the Grand Palais.

"Don't you think that looks like the moment when Seraphine gave a ticket to the little boy for the Ferris wheel?" she said. "You told me the date when they visited the Great Exhibition, so I based my image search on that."

"It does indeed match the scene." Cyrus couldn't see anything beyond the shapes, but filled in the details with his mind. There was Seraphine, in her velvet green coat and bustle skirt, her pile of red hair and gentle smile, bending down to offer kindness to a delighted child. And Lydia, looking on, delighted herself with the first flush of love.

"It's one hell of a coincidence if it's not them, don't you think, Cyrus? How many women can there have been who dressed like that, who fit Lydia's unusual description, in that exact place in Paris on that day?"

"Indeed."

His skeptical brain racked itself for explanations—the photo was planted for him to find, it was fake, the person who wrote the letters—maybe Haydn herself—had seen this photo and taken inspiration from it.

Kathryn seemed to sense his mind working. "You know, it was very difficult to find. I'm not sure I could have found it without my archival training. It required advanced search techniques. It wasn't listed by location or description, only date. I had to research photographers working in Paris that year, and request access to a rather obscure archive."

He was lost in thought when he realized she had more.

"And there's something else," she said. "Marie Vance. There was an M. Vance, who drove an ambulance for the Second Auxiliary Unit, Allied Forces, Souham Barracks, Lille. Look." She showed him a computer printout of another black-and-white photograph. "This is from the French Military Archives. It shows the ambulance, and presumably the driver is M. Vance, but it's too grainy to tell if it's the same person as the Ferris wheel photo. It implies male, but how many ambulance drivers can there have been in one unit? And we can't be sure, but she could easily be the same person as in the photo from the Great Exhibition."

"Any record of what happened to her after the war?"

"Yes." Her eyes shone. "French public death records. 1955. A Marie Vance died in Avenières."

Cyrus breathed deeply. Avenières was the village next to Lydia's mountain.

"It doesn't necessarily prove anything," Kathryn said. "Someone could have built the story around Marie Vance, inserted the clues for you to find, and draw your own conclusions."

Cyrus said, "But I would not have been able to find these clues without your help. And Haydn would know that."

"That's all I could find about Lydia. I think it might require a trip to the Swiss border to find out more. To Avenières. And that's almost impossible. I don't have any travel credits—I used them up visiting a friend in Germany last year."

"Not impossible. I do. Have travel credits, I mean."

"You're not seriously thinking of traveling, Cyrus? In your… condition? It's so dangerous. What happens if it… If it happens and you can't get back…"

"It's a chance I am considering taking. The consequences are greater for that girl, Haydn. She wants us to go together. And she implied to me that she has only one credit."

"So, she wouldn't be able to return easily. Aren't you concerned about her, then? You don't seem to know anything about her. It's funny, I've never seen this Haydn around college. I mean, a girl with bright red hair, tattoos…doesn't ring a bell."

"Do you think I made her up?"

"Did you? Rather a convoluted way to win me back. I hate to say it, but maybe you should find out a bit more about this Haydn. I'm sorry to be suspicious. But what is her real purpose? Is this some overly clever student project? Surely she wouldn't risk traveling just for that?"

"She seems too…kind. For it to be a trick, I mean. She seems to be a good person. And she's not pushy. She wants my help, but she's going to pursue this investigation with or without it."

"And why does she need your help? There's more to this, isn't there? There's something you're not telling me."

He hovered on the brink of telling her about the physics, but something held him back. It would require from Kathryn a leap of faith. If he had not been prepared to do that for his new bride back in 1980, to believe in something he couldn't understand, why should Kathryn do it now, after all the time he had wasted?

Instead, he said, "Well, it appears that deciding whether to look for the house is a question for philosophy. And she seems to be very concerned for me that I find out what happened to my wife." He had crossed the Rubicon of mentioning his wife.

Kathryn lowered her head. "You must have loved her very much. To have never moved on. Sorry…I…I know the Disappearing House is about her."

She touched his hand, and he awkwardly tapped hers in gratitude with his other hand. They were still sitting side by side at the desk, and made a clumsy, shuffling dance of turning their chairs towards each other, so that he felt her kneecaps against his.

"No, it's quite alright. It's true, in a way—I never moved on. I did love her, but not enough. Lydia's letters have shown me that. Lydia really knew how to love unconditionally. Without expecting anything in return. She loved in order to love. She loved based on a profound acceptance of the 'otherness' of her lover. Why couldn't I just believe? I was able to believe in Catholicism—the Holy Trinity, the Virgin Birth, the Resurrection—things that can never be seen or proven." He felt a lump rising in his throat. He was saying too much. "Why couldn't I believe Daphne? For several years after her death, I suppose I mythologized it, and then I abstracted it into a philosophical problem…and now. Well."

Kathryn sighed and rose from her chair to look out of the window at the green quadrangle below, the sea of spires in the distance. Cyrus joined her, and since her arms were folded, he folded his too. It was 11:00, and bells began to peal across the city in a medieval dissonance. When the sound finally died down, Kathryn's voice came as if from far away.

"Sometimes we reserve the cruelty in our hearts for those close to us. I don't know why. Do you know why, Cyrus?"

"Perhaps because we want them to be like us. Mirror images. We cannot see them as separate beings. But Lydia—she accepted that you can never truly possess or understand another person, even the person you love the most."

Dear Carl,

I write to you in the most agitated state. What more can I say about the horrors that continue here? There is only carnage, the aftermath of carnage, and the anticipation of carnage.

No doubt you have read in the newspapers about what they are calling the Second Battle of Ypres. And no doubt they have presented it as a gallant victory, filled with bravery and honor, as if it were nothing more than the Olympic Games. There would be no honor in one hundred thousand dead, even if the whole war had been won. But for what? A few acres of ground? This is collective madness, Carl. Here is the shadow of humanity. Evil is at its head, and we are just automata. There is no other way to be. We are cogs in the wheel of a giant infernal machine.

In my dreams, I see the Ferris wheel of the Great Exhibition morph into grotesque, demonic forms. I see it breaking free from its stays and careering across the battlefield, crushing bodies and leaving mutilated corpses in its wake. Everywhere is fetid mud, infestations of rats and flies, debris of shells and bullets, ruins and rubble from destroyed buildings. They are using poison gas now, you know? This is what chemistry has brought us: an acrid, murderous yellow-green fog that compels us to wear the most dehumanizing masks. There is no option for us to choose the path of morality, for if the soldier's courage falters, they are shot for desertion. I wish I could return to Seraphine, but how can I leave when the other nurses stay?

Thoughts of Seraphine keep me alive, but not sane, because

I have heard nothing, and I am deeply worried. I know she would write if she could, and I freely admit to my bitter jealousy when others receive their letters. Why do hers not get through? Does she look up at the same star every night, as I do? That is one of my feeble consolations. I wonder what is going on in that house, that unwieldy house, while I am away. It was barely under my control while I was there. Did I conjure it from my dreams? My dreams are all nightmares, but my reality is far worse. When will this end? When there are no more young men left?

Carl, I can feel the old intrusions coming back. I am losing myself. I am losing grip on reality. There is chloral hydrate here, but my conscience saves me from it, for how could I take from our limited supplies and deny some poor boy in agony?

Why do you not write, Carl? Are you safe? You doctors are so cunning at getting us to tell everything about ourselves, and yet nothing about what you are feeling. It is so infuriating.

The other nurses all have their sweethearts. Those who do not already have husbands and fiancés already out there fall in love with injured boys. Every so often, we hear the wail of a girl receiving bad news. I am by far the oldest, and while I have never had the slightest maternal instinct, I now feel very protective of them. They look to me to be brave, and I am exhausted from keeping my panic to myself. I do not tell them everything, since most would not approve. And I wear the female uniform, with skirt, blouse, belted coat, and beret—can you imagine?

One day, I let Seraphine's name slip, and I had to pretend she was my daughter. Well, she almost could be. What will we be to each other when I return, I wonder? At my worst moments, I imagine her taking up with that young mahatma

Kumara. They are far more suited, after all, spinning together up there on the astral plane. Perhaps it is selfish of me to think so much of home, but I cannot help feel that it is Seraphine, and not I, who is in great danger.

Your friend,
Lydia

CHAPTER 11

Cyrus

2035

Kathryn came to Cyrus's rooms every day to work on his files for a couple of hours. Sometimes in the morning, then they would have lunch together. Or they would meet with their trays in the Hall, and she would come back to his rooms afterward. Or she would come after dinner, and they would share a glass of whisky in front of the fire. They spent Christmas Day together—"My poor cats, I've completely abandoned them for you," she said—and they joined the muted New Year celebrations together in the Hall.

He asked her if she would prefer him to be out of the way while she worked.

"No, I might need to ask you something. But do tell me if I'm disturbing you."

"No, no, not at all."

She worked with infectious energy, both on his files and her day job. She recruited students to begin dismantling and moving the archives: "We have to get them underground. It's awful, but I rather enjoy the sense of urgency. It's exciting."

Cyrus felt a sense of urgency, too, and he felt he was supposed to do something, say something, but he didn't know how or what. It had been too long; there was too much shame and regret.

One evening, he fell asleep in his chair, and when he woke in the early hours, he found she had put a blanket over him before slipping out. Her perfume lingered. It was the most commonplace and wonderful of revelations. Just when it seemed that life was almost over, it settled effortlessly into a new routine of easy company and pleasure. He felt his flesh coming alive again after decades of mummification. Time had stopped, and their world stood still, he and Kathryn at the point of a zoetrope of chaos that spun around them.

She would sit at a low table in the corner, sometimes looking up and smiling at him.

"I can feel you're watching me, Cyrus."

"You never married," he said.

"That is factually correct."

She didn't look up but flicked through pages with slightly more urgency. Eventually, she broke the silence. "If you want me to elaborate, you will have to ask questions rather than make statements."

"Why did you never marry?"

"Lots of people don't marry. Why didn't you remarry, Cyrus?"

"'Call no man unhappy until he is married,' said Socrates."

Finally, she put down her file with a sigh. "Cyrus. Since you seem to be asking for bold truths. You are the most intelligent man in the world. And the stupidest. 1985. Commemoration Ball. Do you remember?"

His heart lurched at an unwelcome memory. What had he set in motion?

"You were very handsome then."

He remembered her standing on the stone steps on the north side of the quadrangle. It was dusk, the deep violet sky and rotating disco lights, and the flitting people combining into a romantic haze. Or perhaps it was just the sepia of nostalgia, a trick of memory. He remembered the music, a waltz by Satie played by a piano and string quartet. Cyrus had been standing at the fountain, wearing the obligatory tuxedo, affecting a pose with one foot on the fountain, smoking a cigar. How pleased they had been with the silhouette they created, he and his friends. One of them was Roy Lightman.

Kathryn appeared on the stone steps beneath the clock tower. She wore a deep red ball gown. Low cut, shoulders bare, blonde hair tumbling. Was it a red dress? Or was it Lydia's letters confusing her with Seraphine in his mind? Had he considered the possibilities of that moment, the way Lydia had, and then chosen not to go over there, chosen not to dash himself against the rocks? Or had something else prevented him? Memories fought to emerge from some locked box, and those damned letters were only confusing him.

"Well, turning points and all that," Kathryn smiled ruefully. "I ended up going home with Roy Lightman that night. Don't look so shocked. Anyway, that was the end of that. He was a bit of an arse even then."

Roy Lightman. Memories came into focus. Cyrus had been looking over at Kathryn, and his friends noticed.

"See something you like?" said Roy, slapping him on the back. "Absolutely no chance, my friend. She's spoken for—some rower at Keble, I believe. He's from some loaded family—aristocracy. Saw them together only yesterday. Plus, she's known for her sharp tongue—do you really want one of her withering put-downs in front of all these people? Forget it."

Cyrus certainly would be exposing himself to the risk of a humiliating rejection, watched by everyone in this quadrangle that was his whole world. And anyway, he didn't deserve her. He didn't deserve anybody since he had lost Daphne. Five years had passed, and it felt like forever and no time at all.

Jolting himself back to the present, he looked at Kathryn, trying to guess her expression. "So, Roy Lightman broke your heart?"

"No, Cyrus. You did. You were the one who broke my heart." Her voice was matter-of-fact as ever, but she couldn't conceal the crack over the last word.

"I…" He found that his hands were tightly gripping the sides of the armchair, and his face was hot. How terrible, to be faced with the pain one had caused to another. The miserable indignance of it. "And you have held a candle…"

"No, no, not exactly." She turned over papers meaninglessly. "There were others. But no one I was willing to share my life with."

"I… I could never forgive myself, you see…for Daphne. It had only been a few years and… I still hoped she would come back."

"You don't have to explain."

He wished she weren't sitting so far away. He wished she would stop turning over those papers. He wished that one of them would go over to the other. No more of this terrible inertia.

"I do have to explain," he continued. "I can never forgive

myself for my...incredulity. I didn't believe her. If you love someone, surely you should trust them?"

"Perhaps not blindly? Sorry. Poor choice of words. Not unconditionally, I mean. I think you are rather hard on yourself, Cyrus. I don't think she would have wanted you to spend your whole life on this."

"I haven't, not really. I abstracted her, distilled her into a philosophical problem a long time ago. Perhaps it was the mystery I cared about more."

"I'm sure that's not true. But yes, the not knowing must have been close to unbearable. We do insist on knowing everything, don't we?"

"And yet there are some things we are not meant to know." He relaxed a little, back on solid philosophical ground. Maybe he wouldn't need to go over to Kathryn. Maybe he could stay where he was, at a safe distance, with his desk and her low table and the crackling fireplace between them. "I'm rather a fan of Godel's Incompleteness Theorem—there are some things that simply cannot be known. We have only scratched the surface of the universe."

Kathryn laughed. "It doesn't matter anymore. Here we are, two cantankerous old people at the end of the world. You're almost blind, and I have seven cats. A hopeless pair. I don't feel I have wasted my life. And..." She shook herself and patted some folders. "I want to make sure that you haven't wasted yours by sorting out your papers."

But her voice was a little cracked, and she wasn't turning over papers anymore. "Tell me why you care about this so much, Cyrus. Lydia's letters, I mean."

"Please don't ask me."

"If you won't tell me, then I will tell you. This is about your wife. You think that, if you find out what happened to Lydia, you will find out what happened to your wife."

"Tell me why you care about my files so much. It's all nonsense. It's just student essays. Nobody else keeps all their student essays," he returned.

"I care about them because they matter. You are a wonderful teacher, Cyrus. The only reason you haven't published in your lifetime is because you dedicated yourself to your students."

He wasn't sure this was true. His narrative, self-serving into his old age, changed according to his mood. It was either that he had always refused to publish, or that whenever he had planned to publish, something, the universe, had got in the way. And Roy Lightman kept floating to the surface of his memories, unbidden.

Roy Lightman, who had been on the college Publications Committee for thirty years. Who had stood against him for the position of Senior Censor and won. Who said he didn't know Haydn, and yet he did. Roy Lightman, who always wore all white, like that ridiculous Kumara. Who had prevented him from dancing with Kathryn fifty years ago. Cyrus opened the top left drawer of his desk, where he kept the framed photo of him and Daphne—and one other item. A crumpled yellow Post-it. He turned it over and over in his hands, folding and refolding, trying to snap out of his reverie and back into Kathryn's chatter, which was back on safe ground.

"It really would make a wonderful book, Cyrus. I keep thinking of titles. The Disappearing House. The House That Wasn't There. The Ghost House. I know you have written about it too. You just haven't shown me." She looked over at him and smiled, and he could feel the warmth of it, and he smiled back.

"Yes, this house is really coming alive for me as I read all this."

"It's funny," he said, "Lydia's descriptions of the house in her letters really made it come alive, too. In fact, she anthropomorphized it. She said it felt as if the house had a personality all of its own. Perhaps even a malevolent one."

"You're half in another world, Cyrus. What's that in your hands?"

"Ah. I have another Post-it for your collection." He heaved himself into a standing position. He felt on the edge of a cliff. "I'm not sure if it's a story you'll want to tell in your retirement."

"What is it?" She put down her files and came over to the desk. He handed it to her, and she unfurled it carefully and read the scrawled handwriting.

Dear Kathryn. Hope you had fun last night. I'm sorry we didn't get to chat. Would you like to meet for coffee today, 3pm? Yours, Cyrus.

He scanned her face for any sense of recognition, any emotion that he could decipher. He cursed his useless eyes.

"What is it?" she asked.

"1985. I wrote it the day after the Commemoration Ball. I put it in your pigeon hole first thing in the morning, and when I came back later, I saw that you had put it in the waste paper basket."

"No—I didn't. I never saw this note." She was holding it with both hands, shaking her head repeatedly, shaking the note. "I promise, Cyrus. I would have remembered. Because I would have been hoping for a message like this. And I certainly wouldn't have thrown it away like that—you know me—I would have replied."

He thought he might die of regret in that moment. "I don't know whether to laugh or cry."

"Laugh," she said, yet with a tear. "It's one of the few pleasures we have left."

He put his hands tentatively on her upper arms. "I'm sorry. Stupid, blind old man."

She brought her cool, soft hands up to his face. "You are perfectly wonderful. I see it."

"Fifty years of misunderstanding."

"It may be that the whole world is about to end based on a misunderstanding." Kathryn paused. "That's it," she said, suddenly, taking her hands away and stepping back to think.

"What?"

"We've been misunderstanding. It's not Lydia—it's the house. Lydia was not erased from history. It was the house and all traces of it. The house was erased. Something happened in that house."

"Why would someone need to erase all traces of a building?"

"History is littered with things hidden from people by shadowy authorities."

"Oh, I'm not disputing its possibility. I'm thinking out loud."

"What could have been wrong with the house?" said Kathryn. "A shameful crime, a military secret, a scientific discovery?"

"I suppose I'd better tell you the rest of the story. Afterwards, you might want to call our book *The Quantum House*."

Dear Carl,

I write in haste, waiting for the next train to Dijon. If you have news, please leave something for me at the main post office in Geneva, where I will arrive tomorrow. An earthquake, what do you know of it? Of course, we are in the midst of what they are calling the Battle of the Somme, and with the slaughter and mud, there is little time for anything else. But yesterday I came across a week-old Le Matin, and there it was, hidden in the middle pages—an earthquake in the Vuache range! La Mandallaz lies at the very tip of that range, and Chateau de Miroirs lies at the very tip of La Mandallaz. What have I done…

Pray with me, Carl—we must pray to the universe since we have no God—pray that my Seraphine is safe!

Your friend,
Lydia

CHAPTER 12

Cyrus

2035

The glorious novelty of snow. Large flakes were falling with a quiet urgency, and standing at his window with a fire blazing in the grate, Cyrus pressed his forehead to the glass to feel the coolness. He sensed the movement of flakes before his eyes and made out vague colors and shapes behind it—the darkness of a cleared path, two students in colored coats. The static effect mirrored what he saw every time he closed his eyes. He opened the window to catch a flake in his hand and feel it melt. To smell the eerie freshness, hear the world's sounds under their muffled white blanket. He wondered if this would be the last time he would feel snow. In his mind flashed a vision of black flakes swirling instead.

He felt his way back to the leather desk chair and, with a vague sensation of leaping off a cliff—Cyrus had been feeling this a lot recently—he picked up the phone and said, "Call Roy Lightman."

There were plenty of other quantum physicists in Oxford, and yet he felt Roy was the person to ask. He had again the strange sensation that things were unfolding as they should, and that he was powerless to resist. Abandoning himself to fate.

Roy picked up. "Cyrus. How unexpected. What can I do for you? Is everything alright?"

"Yes, yes. I, er, I have a conundrum for you. About quantum physics. Need your help with a little research question."

"I'm intrigued. You're on fire at the moment, Cyrus, what with erasing people from history, and back in the dating game, I see... You're a sly one. The Kathryn saga continues, fifty years on."

Cyrus bristled. Fifty years later, Roy still had the ability to irritate and unnerve him. But here he was, inviting Roy in on an intellectual mystery that belonged to him.

Roy continued, "I'm free now, actually. Probably easier if I come over to your rooms?"

Cyrus didn't want Roy in his rooms, but at the same time, he was forced to admit his limitations. It would take him forever to wrap himself up and then shuffle and feel his way over to Roy's office in the Meadow Building. He didn't want Roy to see him so vulnerable.

"Alright. I'll put the kettle on, shall I?"

They disconnected, and Cyrus boiled the kettle and prepared the tea things. Every ordinary activity like this, he regarded as a rehearsal for when he would have to do it completely blind. He performed the tasks—filling the kettle, placing the teabags, cups, and spoons, selecting biscuits—like a dance, his fingertips alive with sensation. When the table was ready in front of the crackling fire, he stood in the center of the room, unsure which way to turn. He had a sense of, if not a momentous occasion, a thread coming together of something long unraveled.

When the knock came, he hesitated too long so that, by the time he went to open the door, Roy was already pushing at it from the outside, and they collided awkwardly.

"Sorry, old man," said Roy as they shook hands in the center of the room. He chuckled and rocked back and forth on his heels. "What a pair we are. Yin and Yang."

It occurred to Cyrus that he and Roy were mirror images of each other, chiral twins. Cyrus was mostly dressed in black, Roy always in off-white. Both had spent their careers on one problem.

Roy looked around the room at the myriad reflections of himself, endless white figures like beings of light. "God, I'd forgotten about all your mirrors. Must be decades since I was last in here."

Cyrus motioned toward the low table and armchairs. "I've managed to make some tea. Perhaps you'd like to do the honors. I'm getting clumsier by the day."

"How's that going—the, er, blindness?" Roy poured them each a cup of tea.

"Encroaching. It's very strange. I dream these vivid dreams."

"Don't we all."

"Yes, I suppose we're all dreaming about missiles and parabolas and mushroom clouds and bunkers. But my nights are filled with these lurid images, and then each morning when I open my eyes to nothing, I have to remind myself that I can't see."

"I have a friend who went blind last year. Ex-colleague, over at the Korean Institute of Science. Only went and looked at the bloody explosion."

"But he survived?"

"He was at a campus in the far south. Far enough from the epicenter. No doubt the radiation sickness will get him sooner or later. Apparently, a lot of people did the same. We all know the drill—look away from the blast. But we can't help ourselves. It's human nature. We have to know. Moths to the flame, and all that."

Roy blew on his tea and looked around at the wall of shelves filled with the Disappearing House files. Cyrus felt a mixture of emotions—shame at his haphazard file-keeping methodology. Kathryn had made a lot of progress, but there were still piles of ancient, damp box files with scrawled labels, chaotic palimpsests of crossings-out and re-scribbles. Seemingly unconnected themes—murder, Aristotle, psychiatry. And anger at Roy's blocking of his multiple attempts at publication. But did that really happen? Or had he not wanted it enough himself, not tried hard enough to publish? He couldn't tell if Roy was his antagonist, the puppet-master orchestrating Cyrus's whole life, just a bit part, or simply a non-playing character.

Roy said, "A life's work, hey? I have a similar wall in my office, filled with my rantings and ravings and equations."

"Remind me what your specialization is again, Roy."

Cyrus knew very well what it was, and Roy knew that he knew, but they had to continue this old game of belittling each other. "Monopoles, old chap. Single-charge particles, flung out from the beginning of the universe. Most quantum theorists believe they are fundamental particles that have always existed. Others think they split from dipoles at the Big Bang. Symmetry breaking thing. You know."

Cyrus didn't really know. "And what do you think?"

"I think they are two halves of a whole. Upsets my sense of

balance otherwise. And no one has ever seen a magnetic field with a single charge—it doesn't make sense. Simply doesn't work—there have to be two opposing charges. I've spent my career trying to calculate the possibility of two monopoles colliding, and what would happen if they did. Perhaps they are trying to find each other, out there in the universe, each pair like two lost souls."

"And what would happen? If two opposite charges find each other?"

"A bloody big explosion. That's honestly the best layman's takeaway from my research: no one knows what would happen if two monopoles collided. What we do know is that there would be a vast, infinite release of energy."

"Sounds familiar."

"Indeed. Like a bloody nuclear bomb. Mind if I throw a bit more wood on that fire?"

"Please do."

Roy knelt in front of the fire and threw on some logs from the basket. Flames crackled into life and reflected throughout the mirrors. Cyrus noticed Roy struggling to get up and struggling to hide it. His sprightly manner belied the fact that he was over eighty as well.

"The thing is, Cyrus," he said, easing back into his chair, "we don't even know if monopoles are real. No one has ever found one. It was good old Paul Dirac who invented them back in the 1920s, just to fit with an equation. Amazing what humans will do, based on pure belief."

"Do you ever…" Cyrus gulped at the magnitude of the question he was about to ask, but he felt a curious sense of abandon. "Do you ever worry that we have wasted our lives on the wrong thing? Barking up the wrong tree?"

But Roy seemed unsurprised and unfazed. "No, not at all. The quest for knowledge is valuable in itself. And I think that an idea will have its time when it's ready."

"Is that why you refused to publish any of my papers?" There, he had said it. There was a pause, and Roy's face darkened for a moment, or was that just Cyrus's imagination? But then, to his astonishment, he didn't deny it.

"No, that was pure pettiness. Spite. Everyone is motivated by spite, Cyrus. And that's why we are where we are. The world is run on vindictiveness. Nasty little men swinging their dicks around. Whichever side is the most vindictive will... Well, nobody will win. That's the point. But, you know, ultimately perhaps it wasn't me but the universe that decided not to publish your research. Perhaps it wasn't yet time for your ideas. Paradigm shifts happen when they happen. Like a tutorial—you take the students on a journey, and you don't reveal the critical point, the plot spoiler, until they've had time to think for themselves. We keepers of knowledge only grant access when a person is ready."

Cyrus pondered it. "Wait without thought, for you are not ready for thought."

"What's that, old man?"

"T.S. Eliot. The man has a quote for every occasion." Cyrus leaned forward and used every ounce of concentration he had to take a sip of tea, replace the wobbling cup, and gingerly push the plate of biscuits towards Roy. *Mind-body problem indeed*, he thought. If only his intellect could override his failing body, his aching spirit. "So, ideas have to wait for their time. Perhaps I'll take it as a compliment that you think I am in possession of some paradigm shift for which the world isn't ready."

"Who knows, Cyrus. Maybe your Disappearing House is the

key to the universe. The still point in the turning world—there's some more T.S. Eliot for you."

Cyrus knew Roy was being facetious, but still. What an admission about the publications. What a revelation, that human beings weren't so complicated—they were all motivated by love, hate, jealousy, spite, pity. He wanted to say, "And I suppose it was pettiness that made you steal Kathryn from me." But what would be the point? It was time to get to the question of the house, despite his mistrust of Lightman. Roy would not believe this was an academic question. There was enough bad blood between them, and Cyrus had enough academic arrogance that he would never ask for Roy's help with a philosophical conundrum. But if it wasn't an academic question, what was it?

Should I look at an invisible house?

What would that mean for Daphne?

If...Haydn was right?

He took a deep breath. "Here's my question, Roy. Let's say you have an object in superposition. Like Schrodinger's cat. But not a cat...a...let's say a house. And the options are not just alive or dead, but... Well, let's say there are several options. And you want to look at it, but you know that the act of looking at it will propagate this house into one of these options...and some are... preferential over others. Is there a way of predicting the most likely outcome? Can you calculate it?"

Roy leaned back in the chair, rubbing his hand over his mouth, looking into space, and shaking his head slightly. Although Cyrus couldn't see clearly, he could sense the affectation, the theatrical amusement and irritation at his uninformed question, and he knew he would have to endure Roy's condescension before he got anywhere near an answer.

"You see," Roy finally began, "this is the problem with modern physics. At the limits of human understanding, we must rely on metaphor and imagery, so we get tangled up with cats and spooky action and multiverses, analogies that are, in fact, very misleading. Schrodinger should never have gone with the cat—it's a nasty little metaphor—but the main problem is that a cat is not a quantum object. Quantum physics applies at the quantum level. But a cat is a macroscopic object, and it can't be in superposition. Its wave function would immediately collapse since it interacts with its environment, destroying the quantum effects. It's called decoherence."

"But could you have a macroscopic object that doesn't interact with its environment?"

"If you were able to fully isolate it from air, gravity, light, sound, everything, then in theory, yes. If it were invisible, for example. I mean, in the thought experiment, the cat is in theory, isolated, invisible. But in reality, it's impossible."

Cyrus said, "But in the experiment, the cat is a quantum object because we can't see it. It's only the act of looking at it that causes it to be one thing or the other. And that is decoherence, right? That's when the wave function collapses, and it becomes the one thing or the other. And yet—forgive me if I am misunderstanding—the paradox is that a system does not change while you are observing it."

"Where are you going with this, Cyrus?" Roy shifted in his chair. His tone of derision couldn't mask his interest.

"At the precise moment when you are observing something, it does not change. So, what happens if you observe it many times? Infinite times?"

"I presume you are leading me towards the quantum Zeno effect? Tell me what you think it is," Roy said.

"What I understand by the quantum Zeno effect refers to the slowing down of time through multiple observations. A system cannot change while you are watching it, so if you look at it enough times, you can freeze it in its initial state. You just keep on looking at it so it can never change."

"Sort of. A decent layman's description. But when you say slowing down time, we're talking about Plank seconds—tiny fractions of seconds."

"Yes. But what about if you look at it infinite times?"

"How can you look at something infinite times?" Roy had lost his air of amusement now and looked at Cyrus intently.

Cyrus hesitated and then jumped off the cliff. "With mirrors. Two mirrors looking at each other into infinity."

Roy paused. "Okay. So, in this thought experiment, you have convinced me that, if we were to have an invisible house, it could be a quantum object. And if we were to look at this invisible house an infinite number of times, it could be placed into a superposition, an unchanging and unspecified state. Now what?"

"What would then happen if someone from outside the system were to look at the house. Collapse the waveform, force the house out of superposition into a possible existence. I believe there is something called the Born rule? A way of calculating the probabilities of what it might then become?"

Roy paused again before saying, "I see you've gone deep, man. But the Born rule applies to the smallest particles in the universe, which have very few options. They can oscillate in one of two directions. The whole universe is based on whether particles oscillate one way or another. And even at this very limited level, the outcomes are inherently probabilistic. We can calculate likelihoods, but the outcome of a single observation is random. We would then have to repeat the experiment multiple times to eventually come out with the calculated probability."

Cyrus nodded. "Yes, I see. A cat can be either alive or dead. One thing or another. But a house can be all sorts of things. There, not there, ruined, renovated, inhabited, empty…"

"And I imagine in your *experiment*, you can't look at the house multiple times and take an average. You look once, and that's what it is forever. No margin for error."

"I see. I mean, I suppose I knew. I'm on that strange fluid border between physics and philosophy, and I suppose I was looking for a bit of rigor."

"Oh, quite right to ask, old man. We physicists can make up an equation for just about anything. We're utterly cavalier. But I think with this, you've come back around into the realms of moral philosophy."

"Indeed. It's a moral question. Based on incomplete knowledge, what would be the right thing to do? What are the risks?"

Roy said, "It's all about temptation, isn't it? What do humans historically do when faced with temptation? Pandora's box, Eve and the apple, Icarus and the sun, Orpheus looking back at Eurydice. Mythology has always warned humans not to look, and temptation was always too great for us. We can't help ourselves."

"The same for your friend in Korea. Same for Oppenheimer and his pals at Los Alamos. Because let's face it, they didn't invent the nuclear bomb to stop a war, to save the world from evil. A bomb to stop a war is a contradiction in terms. Men invented the bomb to see if they could. The vaulting ambition to know. They wanted to believe they could. So it's all about what we are prepared to believe."

"Indeed," Roy said. "They didn't know for sure they weren't

going to trigger the end of the world when they tested that bomb at Los Alamos. But they still did it."

"In a sense, they did trigger the end of the world. Just with a longer timeline."

They were quiet then, each deep in thought, until a rogue ember from the fire crackled into life, dislodging a burning log which tumbled onto the carpet. Roy grabbed the iron poker and began beating at it, with unnecessary force, as Cyrus looked on, helpless.

CHAPTER 13

Cyrus

2035

"What is time?"

It was ironic that this tutorial was scheduled for today, when Cyrus felt the march of time in so many ways. Winter had come and gone. Winters had been getting shorter for decades, but this year in particular, the Earth seemed eager to get to the spring that might be its last. And it was finally spring. He could not see it, but he could smell the new freshness and hint of warmth in the air, the new quality of light like a false promise. The curious limbo of the winter months replaced by a nervous acceleration.

He was almost completely blind now. Only the memory of sight remained. The degeneration in his sight had been exponential, and there were little more than shadows left now. After throwing down the gauntlet of his question, he leaned on the high window ledge and looked out, not wishing to face his students with those pale, useless eyes. Not wanting to face Haydn, who lurked around his life like a harbinger of doom. He felt a curious flippancy on behalf of these young people. What did any of this matter, how could they bring themselves to care… And yet they did.

Numbers were dwindling. There was no talk of officially closing the universities and schools, but the advice was to be within four minutes of a shelter entrance, so many students had opted to go home to their families. His seminar room was half full. He could not see the individual faces, but he could see the empty spaces where bodies should be. Bodies that had understandably chosen to be elsewhere.

Some students had joined the volunteer forces—fire brigades, medical teams, shelter managers, builders, cooks. Others had returned to be near their families, to be four minutes from a shelter entrance, as instructed. He would keep on doggedly teaching those who still had hope, who still wanted to keep on learning until the bitter end, trying to work out what it felt like to be alive in this time.

Receiving no answers, Cyrus continued, "Humans have puzzled over time for millennia. Some would argue that since Einstein and the advent of the quantum revolution, our understanding of time has undergone a significant transformation. Others would say that it hasn't fundamentally altered at all. The theory of relativity teaches us that there is no absolute time; it is relative to the observer. However, in psychological terms, we have always known that."

He decided to risk moving away from the lectern and left one hand on it to steady himself as he shuffled into the space in front of the students. There would be no more flourishes of his gown, darting to the window, striding down the aisle. But he could move forward and backward, one foot in front of the other, his motion stimulating their thoughts and his.

"Aristotle defined time as a measure of change in terms of

'before' and 'after.' He argued that time cannot exist independently of change or motion, making it a relational concept. And St. Augustine famously said, 'What then is time? If no one asks me, I know what it is. If I wish to explain it to him who asks, I don't know.' He goes on to explore the subjective nature of time and introduces the idea of 'psychological time,' suggesting that past, present, and future exist in the mind as memory, attention, and expectation. That isn't far from modern post-quantum theories of time. Physicists have had all sorts of avant-garde theories about time. Quantum physics has all sorts of possibilities, as long as we can find its equations.

"Fundamentally, it is all about our obsession with measurement. Our desperate need to quantify things that perhaps cannot be quantified, or at least not by our human cognitive standards." Cyrus put out a hand to find the lectern, and it flailed in the air for a moment before touching the wood. "Here is a further question. Does it matter if we understand time or not? Since our experience of time is fundamentally subjective."

One student said, "I would argue that it matters more than anything. Understanding time is like understanding God."

Another replied, "Then perhaps it is something we should not understand."

"So what is time?" Cyrus continued. "We can define a second formally, according to an atomic clock, as the duration of nine billion oscillations of a cesium atom. And we can measure the age of the universe as thirteen point eight billion years, with remarkable accuracy, by using cosmic observations and the speed of light. But is it arbitrary, our determination to measure things? Perhaps, but it is understandable. Because it is temporality that makes us human. The certainty of our own mortality, the race against time to live our lives. Heidegger introduced the idea of 'being-toward-death' as a way of understanding human temporality and argued that our experience of time is grounded in our finite, mortal nature. What would we be without this race against time?"

Cyrus wondered how much his teaching of time had been influenced by Lydia's letters. She had been experiencing her own crisis of temporality that was entangled with the waning days of the Belle Epoque, the coming of the First World War, and the love of someone who appeared to live on another temporal plane entirely. There seemed to be an acceptance, depressingly familiar, amongst all concerned in her letters, all the characters, that war was coming one way or another. And he wondered what the phrase "race against time" meant for these young people. How long would they have? Months, days, years? It would be better not to know.

They delved into modern philosophy of time, which was tangled up with quantum physics, the subject for which he had always felt unqualified, and now was forced to try and understand. Cyrus continued. "Newton's universe was a three-dimensional space containing material objects, and a History of the Universe was a dynamic process that unfolded in time. God, looking from the outside, would see the Universe coming into being one stage at a time. But a new vision of time took shape with the advent of relativity. This new vision presented space and time together as a four-dimensional manifold of events. In this universe, there is no ontological difference between here and there, then, now, and the future. This is often called the 'block universe' theory. The past, present, and future exist simultaneously as part of a four-dimensional shape. Events are points, and no moment has a privileged status as the present. Every moment exists whether there is someone to observe it.

There is no 'flow of time.' It's not an arrow. What is 'now' for one observer may be 'past' or 'future' for another. It sounds very modern, but it echoes an ancient philosophical debate between Heraclitus, who argued that 'all is flux,' and Parmenides, who said that 'change is an illusion.'

"So, it seems that humans have always had an inkling that the human linear view of time may not be accurate. Is it perhaps a survival mechanism? Perhaps we can only see time as an arrow. Perhaps we can only see time unfold like a piece of music, from one moment to the next."

Cyrus tried to create a mental timeline of his own life and found that he couldn't. How could one bear to contemplate all those wasted years? One could only think in terms of linear time, but how could one process the millions of discrete moments that made up a life, one after another? In particular, now that his past was coming back to encroach upon his present, and that an uncertain future was dragging him forward with invisible iron chains.

"What do you think?" he asked the students. "Could we live with any other structure of knowledge, for example, retro-causality—the future affecting the past? What if the whole paradox of our lives is that they are built around time, and yet time doesn't exist?"

"Like a god," someone said.

"Exactly. It's all about what we are prepared to believe. What if time were a god?"

Hands went up. One student said, "If the future were able to affect the past, surely it would prevent bad things from happening? Preventable things?"

"Ah," said Cyrus, "but you are making two important assumptions there. Firstly, you are assuming that whatever force is acting on us from the future, human or otherwise, is a benevolent force. Secondly, you are assuming that things are preventable. A pandemic triggered by a lone incident in a laboratory may be preventable, but war—some would argue that war is an inevitable part of history."

"What does all this say about free will?" asked the Eton boy. "Doesn't it mean everything is meaningless?"

"I don't think it necessarily negates free will. To use a clumsy analogy from quantum physics—forgive me, Haydn, our resident physicist—what happens inside an atom is probabilistic. Isn't that correct? Every microparticle does its own thing, and we can only make predictions. But it all comes together. A quantum computer is extremely reliable, but each tiny qubit within it does its own thing. A very crude analogy, but is it a way of considering that we might have free will as individuals?"

Haydn nodded. "Yes, I suppose. All of us humans each doing our own thing? Although…"

The Eton boy spelled out what they were all thinking, looking down at his desk. "I'm not feeling an awful lot of free will at the moment. Don't know about you."

"No, indeed," said Cyrus.

Free will. What a thing to discuss, when they were all about to be either annihilated or forced underground.

"I think it means that the moment matters." It was Haydn. Did he hear emotion in her voice for the first time?

She continued, "The moment is everything. We can use Zeno's arrow again. The paradox of duration—how can duration be composed of instants that are durationless? Therefore, we can only live moment by moment."

"Very good." Cyrus felt Haydn's eyes boring into him, as if imploring him to *live in the moment.* "Putting aside the physics of it, can we imagine a point outside time? If we could see all time at once, what would we do differently? If I had a God's eye view of time, I would make sure no one else did. I would do whatever is required to conceal the Archimedean point from the rest of the world. We must not know. We must believe that time exists. For without urgency, there is no yearning." *Lydia.* Lydia had said this. How many times, he wondered, had he plagiarized her in his lectures? "What would you change, if you had perfect knowledge?"

"I think there can be no worse purgatory than to be able to see the future," said someone. "Or the past, for that matter. Imagine having the perfect memory."

"There are some things we'd rather forget."

The class drew to a close, and as the students filed out towards the sun, Cyrus waited for Haydn. Her hair was no longer a beacon to his eyes, as he had now lost colors as well, and he had to guess as he called out "Haydn." There was a slightly desperate waver to his voice that he loathed. He could sense from her body language that she was still a little reproachful.

"I haven't been able to solve your problem, Haydn. I don't know what would happen if we looked at the house. I don't know if I believe anything you have told me. But I will go to the mountain with you."

Her stance instantly softened. "Really?" She was gratified, and so was he. Excited even at the sudden prospect of adventure. Sudden because he had not decided until that very moment.

"Really. I want to see it again. I mean… You will need to be my eyes. Can you…make the arrangements?"

"Yes, I'll register you for the conference. Thank you,

Professor Field." She bounced on the balls of her feet, and he thought for a moment she might put her arms around him, but she darted from the room with a new energy.

Events were still going ahead in hope. Concerts planned for next year in the purest expression of optimism, athletes still training for the Olympics. Students still learning.

And Cyrus was going back to the bridge.

Cyrus and Kathryn sat opposite each other at the end of a long table in the hall, their lunch trays touching. It was a daily ritual. He needed her help now and couldn't imagine how he would manage if she were not with him. But she seemed to enjoy his company, and he tried to grasp how good that felt. A group of students sat further down the table, and he overheard them discussing dresses, arrangements, tickets.

"It's the Commemoration Ball tomorrow," he said.

"That is factually correct."

"Yes… I'm very glad that it's going ahead. The young people need these things. And the old people."

Kathryn put down her knife and fork. "Cyrus. Are you asking me to the ball?"

"Yes. I believe I am."

He felt the warmth of her smile.

"Perhaps we could recreate that moment from 1985. With me on the steps."

"I wouldn't be able to see you this time."

"Do you know something funny? I still have that dress. I might even wear it. I'm still about the same size. What do you think?"

"I think you should."

The next evening, they walked out into the quad under a violet sky. Fifty years since the last Commemoration Ball, and the college had tried to recreate it exactly—the same piano and string quintet, same stage and disco lights, same balloon displays, gold disc dancefloor, buffets, photo booths, fireworks. People flocked in groups of tuxedos and taffeta. The mood was of last day's decadence.

Cyrus and Kathryn maneuvered through the crowd and found themselves a space on the gold disc. The quintet struck up Satie's "Je Te Veux." He took one of her hands, put the other on her bare shoulder, and she held his waist. They laughed at their old-fashioned waltz position, laughed in the knowledge that students were whispering about them.

"I suppose we must look rather sweet," said Kathryn. They danced in silence for a while, cheeks lightly touching, and for Cyrus, the world was Kathryn and Kathryn was the world.

"I must have done something good in a previous life," he said, suddenly. "To be here with you now. After all my mistakes. I don't know what on earth you see in me."

"More than you see in yourself. And anyway...you can't choose who you love. I suppose I didn't choose you. The universe did."

They swayed to the Parisian nostalgia of Satie's gentle waltz, and although he couldn't see them, Cyrus imagined a clear sky of stars above them. Not satellites or airplanes, but stars, unfettered by human light. Real light, from the beginning of the universe.

Eventually, she asked, "How long do you have, Cyrus?"

"How long do any of us have?"

"I mean, before you go completely blind."

"I don't know. But…it's accelerating. The degeneration, I mean."

"When the sirens go…" she began.

"When the sirens go…we could go together," he finished.

"You mean, stay together. Up here. There are no places down there for people like us."

"No, indeed not. Kathryn. Do you believe there are souls destined to be together, like two parts of a whole?"

"No. Not exactly. But do I believe the person for me exists? Yes."

Cyrus swallowed. "I'm sorry. That I couldn't be more like Lydia. I was afraid to seize the moment. Afraid to dash myself against the rocks."

"Oh, please don't do that. Sounds awfully painful."

"It's something that Lydia wrote."

"I'm sorry, too. For what happened to Daphne. For how it affected your life."

"I could never forgive myself, you see. For not believing. I don't want to make the same mistake again. That's why I have to…" He couldn't say it, couldn't tell her he was going to go.

"Perhaps we are destined to make the same mistakes again. Just come back to me, Cyrus. If you can."

He looked into her eyes with everything he had left.

"I know you're going to go," she said. "And I know I can't stop you."

"If you don't want me to go, I won't. I'll stay here with you."

"No. You should go. If there's even a chance that you might find your answer, you should go. And as for us, if our last days are coming, I want them to be like this. Not in terror and pain, not in darkness or a blinding flash of light. Just like this, together, in the moment."

They moved amongst bodies. He felt Haydn was there somewhere, always watching him, a ticking clock. He would soon be completely blind. The world was disappearing into a vignette surrounded by blackness. Every day he was further down the tunnel away from reality. But in some ways, he felt he had never seen the world more clearly. The horror of a wasted life had softened into the wistfulness of regret, and then into the possibility of hope. In a world devoid of hope, there was this moment, and perhaps that was all that mattered, and perhaps everything was unfolding exactly as it should.

"Do you know something else funny?" he said. "Here we are at the end of the world, and I have never been this happy."

Dear Carl,

It is all gone—nothing, nothing! The mountain has moved and taken her with it. I will die, I will die here, I cannot live, I cannot breathe.

Early this morning, I begged a carriage to take me from Geneva to Avenières, which was cloaked in a thick mist. From my position in the chaise, I could barely see the horses two meters in front of me as we jolted up the mountain. I arrived in the village in the most frantic state, grabbing at people, women in their doorways, children at the fountain in the square. But they were as automata and could tell me nothing. The village did not seem damaged by the earthquake, but certainly by the war. It seemed half-dead.

How to get to the Chateau des Miroirs? To run would take too long, even though I would run a thousand miles for Seraphine. I saw a horse tethered outside the inn, and I simply took it. After I mounted, it whinnied and reared up on its hind legs a few times, not so much in protest as in solidarity at the urgency of our mission. We galloped through the mist. It had no saddle or bridle, so I held on to its hair. But after a time, I could sense fear in the horse, and it eventually stopped, sooner than I had expected. I realized we were already at the edge of the cliff—the cliff had moved. Had I been running, I should have continued into the void.

A piece of the mountain has simply fallen away and taken my house with it. It was a clean break, as if the cliff had been sheared by a giant scythe. I fell down and lay on my stomach, face over the void, trying to see what was below, but there was nothing but thick mist, with a yellow-green tint, like the battlefield. I screamed her name, Seraphine, Seraphine, into the abyss, but my words echoed back to me. No doubt the echo came from that infernally smooth fault mirror on the other side. Even if I could not see it, it could see me, hear me. It knows everything. And it has taken her. She has gone, she has gone.

Oh, Carl, why will you never tell me what I should do? What should I do? I searched the whole mountain for a way down, scrabbling my way along the edge, lying down on my front again and again to peer into the void. My skirt and blouse were soaked in muddy water, and the mist seeped into my bones so that I was shivering in June. But there was no possible point of access—it is a sheer drop. Somewhere down there is my house…my love.

It is as if she were never here, as if I imagined the whole thing, the realest thing in my life. You know how I used to have visions, Carl. Tell me that this was all a vision, too—Seraphine, La Mandallaz, the fault mirror—all of it. For if it was indeed real, then it means I have killed her, I who brought her here to live on a mountaintop in the middle of nowhere.

If I had only stayed in Paris, remained blind, bathed in frivolity, decadence, meaninglessness—then she would still be alive. What does that mean? What can it mean?

And what if the earthquake happened during a meditation, when she was up in the astral plane? From what I understand, it did happen in the evening. What would it mean to have your physical body die while your soul is up there, attached only by the silver thread? Did her soul die too, or is she trapped in purgatory forever? That is the only thought that keeps me from throwing myself over the edge. That was always her dream to go crashing into the abyss. She manifested it as much as I manifested the house.

The horse had bolted in fear, so I staggered back to Avenières on foot, a mess of tears and mud. I don't think I have cried so much, or at all, since I was in your hospital ward. I am now staying at the inn. That evening, the mist cleared, and the navy sky was lit with stars, like a billion tears.

She is here somewhere, I know it. I shall stay here forever. Even if she never reveals herself to me, I believe she is here, and that is enough. I will live on the memory of what we had, and I will never leave this place without her.

Yours,
Lydia

CHAPTER 14

Cyrus

2035

Cyrus's age and vulnerability were a great help on the journey—they passed checkpoint after checkpoint with little interrogation. He felt curiously childlike, an innocent old man being cared for and guided. They changed trains at London and took the Eurostar to Paris, changing there for Geneva. He took in as much as he could with his other senses, allowing himself to be completely dependent on Haydn. He felt in danger, yet at the same time, he trusted that her intentions, while dishonest, were ultimately good. He felt he had very little time left. He thought constantly about having left Kathryn. Her extraordinary generosity in accepting his otherness, in allowing him to go without her. Instead of the remote possibility of a life underground, she chose to let him have this moment.

The train rattled on. He could only imagine the rushing of fields and forests, Haydn occasionally describing to him something of interest that they passed. He thought of Lydia, who must have taken a similar route back from the battlefields to her mountain, in desperate anticipation, not knowing yet that a portion of it had disappeared. Not knowing that she might never see Seraphine again.

They were quiet for a long time. The motion of the train and his forehead against the window, put Cyrus in a contemplative, confessional mood. Haydn's walls had still not come down, and he felt he should get to know this strange girl on whom he had staked everything.

"What about your parents, Haydn? You never told me much about your family. Are they still in Switzerland?"

"No. They were in Seoul."

"I'm sorry. Where were you when it happened?" Until now, he had viewed Haydn not as a real person but as a sort of angel of death. Not of the insidious kind, more like one of those beings that leads someone gently towards their end. A Dickensian ghost of the past.

"It's okay. I was in Switzerland, finishing school. I immediately flew to the UK. I didn't really have a plan, other than to get as far away from the fallout zone as possible. I thought of going to the US eventually. But obviously, nowhere is safe now. I'm good at taking care of myself. What about you? Family?"

"No, just me." He thought of Kathryn. "My family is the Disappearing House problem, and the students who help me."

"When did you realize you were going to dedicate your whole career to the question?"

"I don't think I ever did, really. I was angry with Daphne for a very long time, you know. When she disappeared, she stole our future. It isn't something one ever gets over. I was investigated, of course. When a woman disappears, suspicion is quite rightly placed on the husband or boyfriend. There was no evidence of course, while there was evidence of her travelling back to Switzerland while I was far away in France, still on our honeymoon. Water-tight alibi. At the time, it felt laughable to me that I should ever need to use the word 'alibi.' Even after the investigation closed, a cloud still hung over me. There were always people who believed that I must have done it. Because what are the chances? I replayed it so many times in my mind. I went back there a hundred times."

"Well, you did much more than that. I mean, I presume you started this Disappearing House problem to try and figure out what might have happened."

"It wasn't as conscious or as simple as that, but yes, I suppose. Because I knew Daphne—perhaps not as well as I had thought—but she was a kind person, and she did love me. She would never have disappeared forever without some sort of explanation. She had been planning to come back. She wasn't mentally ill. Something happened to her."

Suddenly, a commotion erupted in the aisles, accompanied by cries of *"Take to the streets... It's all lies... Don't go underground...!"* followed by gasps and struggles, and a sense of being buffeted. After the carriage door slammed, Haydn explained, "A protester, and two policemen. I think he's from Apocalypse Now."

"Ah. A rare sighting then—most of them have been rounded up."

"Do you think every generation believes it's the end of the world?" she asked after a while. "Like, we all think we have a monopoly on the apocalypse?"

"I know what you mean, but no. I think this time might be it. I have lived eighty-five years. I have seen the cycles."

The atmosphere in the carriage settled once again, and Haydn resumed their thread. "So why philosophy? What made you think that would contain the answer?"

"Well, for starters, I was already a junior lecturer in philosophy when Daphne went missing. And we all choose a best-fit narrative, don't we? But it did seem to be a philosophical problem more than anything else. There had to be a logical solution. I replayed it in my head so many times that I started to believe, and then I began to question my memory. Perhaps it hadn't happened the way I remembered it. Battling to keep her memory alive was distorting it. So, handing it over as a philosophy problem allowed me to step outside it. And year after year, students made it something else entirely. It had become itself. Something abstract."

"Perhaps the answer is there, among those files," Haydn said. "Because there must be an answer, doesn't there? Perhaps we'll find out now. There has to be an answer to everything."

"Does there? Maybe the human quest for knowledge has done more harm than good. My life has been one of yearning, and I don't know if that's a good or a bad thing."

"Maybe it is you playing a trick on me, Professor Field. Maybe you wrote those letters. As some sort of elaborate alibi. And I found them." There was a pause, and he could tell she regretted her words, had perhaps gone too far. But it was a reasonable suggestion, and had often come up over the years—the husband did it. Suggesting he was responsible for a disappearance that he did in fact believe himself responsible for—it somehow moved him further away from blame, took away some of the guilt.

"Like I said, I was investigated for her death. Men kill their wives all the time. When a woman dies, it is usually a close relation. And there were no other suspects..."

The train pulled into Dijon, and a flurry of passengers, bags, and announcements ensued. He couldn't see it, but he felt it—

the heightened anxiety in the air. Everyone was trying to get to where they were supposed to be, an innate collective sense that something was about to happen.

His phone rang. It was Kathryn.

"Hello, Cyrus. How's the journey going?"

Her voice sounded strange, and he took her off speaker phone and put the device to his ear. "Very well. No problems with checkpoints so far, and we should be in Geneva by the evening."

"Is she there with you?" The way Kathryn said "she" was loaded with meaning.

"Yes."

"Can she hear?"

"No, I don't think so."

"Cyrus. Haydn Young is not a student at the university."

"Ah, I see." He tried to remain nonchalant, to betray no emotion as his mind reeled.

"I read her Disappearing House essay, and I thought it was excellent—unquestionably one to include in the anthology. So, I did as I have with the other student essays we selected. I looked up her contact details. No one by the name of Haydn Young is a member of this college, of the philosophy faculty, the physics faculty, or the university."

His mind raced for explanations. She just wanted to learn. She was a lonely orphan. She had these letters and needed a way to get to Cyrus. She was planning to tell him. He looked toward the innocent face sitting opposite him, and felt her smiling back. But he knew from the quality of the silence on the line that there was more to come.

"I searched for her online, obviously. Cyrus, Haydn Young

doesn't exist. It's a fake name. Whoever she is, it's someone else."

He felt a curious *déjà vu.* Lydia wiped from the past, Haydn wiped from the present..

"And this conference—I don't think it exists. I looked it up, and there is a website, but it's strangely lacking in detail. I'm not convinced. Why would there be a philosophy conference at a time like this?"

"Well, I'm not sure we ever had any intention of going…"

"Still. I'm calling you to say be careful, Cyrus. There's more to this. I wish I could come to you. So come back to me, if you can."

He hung up and placed his forehead against the window to feel the vibrations. All he could see was a general rushing. When he closed his eyes, the rushing continued behind his lids. He still felt that he was being led towards some sort of judgment, and he must see it through. He didn't want to face this new development. But the silence between them was different now.

"Everything ok?" asked Haydn. "Who was that?"

"Who are you, Haydn?"

"You can't just believe I am who I say I am?'

"I know you're not a student."

She studied his face. "You think this is some sort of plot."

"I know it is some sort of plot."

"So that is what the phone call was about, then?"

Cyrus didn't respond. She didn't care to elaborate, and he didn't care to push it.

They arrived in Geneva, and after a long, hot wait at the security checkpoint, Haydn maneuvered him into a taxi that took him to their hotel. Exiting the cab, he felt cobblestones under his feet, the swish of a revolving door, and smelled the fresh scent of lake.

"It's odd. This place feels familiar," he said. "Now that my sight has failed, the images in my head are taking over, and all I can picture is the hotel I stayed in with Daphne. It's the same time of year, as well."

"*Bienvenus à l'Hotel des Armures,*" said a porter who took his bag.

"Hotel des Armures. It *is* the same hotel. Did you know that, Haydn?"

"No. How could I? It was just the only hotel available. Most are already closed. Will it be okay?"

"Yes, yes. It's just remarkable—how the body knows."

Later that evening, he felt his way out to the balcony of his room to breathe in the cool night air. He bathed in the sounds of voices in the street, the distant rush of the Jet d'Eau on the lake, and the occasional car pulling up to the reception down below. He thought of Kathryn. He marveled at his new heightened senses, the way he could distinguish the smells of gasoline, food cooking, algae from the lake, early summer tree pollen. And he could smell the subtle perfume of Haydn behind him, although he had known she was there even before that.

"Sometimes I feel you are coming just before you arrive," he said, without turning round. "And when I am talking to you, I feel as if I am talking to myself."

She came up alongside him, and they both placed their hands on the balcony rail.

"I just wanted to see if you needed anything. It's been a long day."

"I'm perfectly fine. But thank you. You look after me very well, Haydn."

"The lights in the sky are different tonight," she said. "I don't know if you can make anything out. But I think they are real stars up there. I think that's Orion."

"I imagine you haven't seen many real stars in your lifetime with all the satellites. Constellation of technology. Just glowing debris, most of them."

"Stars are glowing debris as well, I suppose. I love to think about the way light travels. That star up there—let's say it is Rigel, I'm not sure—I'm looking at it as it was a million years ago. If someone were looking at us from up there, right now, they might see dinosaurs or the Roman Empire, or the Hundred Years' War, depending on how far away they are."

"Tell me you're a physicist without telling me."

"That's how I got into physics, looking up at the sky. What does it mean, Cyrus, that we can see real stars tonight?"

"I think they have turned off the satellites."

"And what does that mean?" She sounded afraid, childlike, and for the first time, he felt it his role to comfort and protect.

"It means, I fear, that we are closer than ever. Someone is about to make the first move."

CHAPTER 15

Cyrus

2035

Haydn rented a car the next morning. Cyrus felt giddy, standing in the rental car office while she made the arrangements. They would possibly never return this car, and the assistant didn't seem to care. Haydn drove them the thirty minutes of winding roads to Avenières. He could feel the land rising in its twists and turns, marvelling at the way his body sensed the change in altitude.

"Here we are," she said finally, turning off the engine. "This is the main square of Avenières. In fact, we can't seem to drive any further. The road is blocked by a red-and-white barrier up ahead. It just ends. As if this village is the last place on earth." Mid-morning, and it was already hot. He felt the blazing sun lighting up the shadows in his eyes. He breathed in deeply, and behind the scents of early Alpine summer—flowers and high grass—he sensed a hint of sulphur that took him back almost sixty years.

"It's very quiet, as you can hear," said Haydn. "Almost deserted, like a ghost town. Ours is the only car in the square, and most of the buildings seem to be abandoned and boarded up."

"What about the *mairie?*"

"It's across the square, but it's closed. Looks derelict, as if it hasn't been functioning for some time."

"Oh dear, that was our best hope of finding local records."

"There is a bar, though, and it seems to be open. L'Auberge du Terroir."

"That's the one from Lydia's letters. Describe it to me."

They walked across the main square. Cyrus knew it was the main square without her description, because he felt the cobblestones under his feet, and they had to swerve to avoid the central fountain. And he knew it was the main square because he had been there before, in 1980, and '81, and '82, asking and asking. It was not difficult to picture the Auberge, a seventeenth-century inn with faded signs and Belle Epoque lettering.

Haydn guided him through the door, and he immediately felt the cool of darkness behind his eyelids, a dark shadow over the blurred film of his vision. He heard low French voices, the odd clink of glass, and he smelled damp tobacco and stale wine. Haydn maneuvered him into a booth. She had naturally fallen into describing his surroundings for him. "Okay, there's a lady at the bar, and five old guys at a table playing cards. I'll go and get us a drink."

So vulnerable did Cyrus feel, alone in the booth, that he sensed his time rapidly draining away.

"Vous venez d'ou, monsieur?"

He realized that the men at the card table were speaking to him. The voice sounded friendly. He replied in French, aware of his strong English accent. "I am from England. I'm with my student, Haydn." He motioned vaguely in the direction she had gone. "We are doing some research."

"Quel type de recherches?"

He felt the absurdity of saying philosophy. Who would be researching philosophy at a time and in a place like this? And in any case, it wasn't quite true. They were looking for someone. "We are looking for a person," he explained. "A woman who lived here long ago. She died in 1955."

"I was born in 1955!" said a voice, and there was laughter and in-jokes as they reminisced about ageing.

"We thought we might try the *mairie* and look at the local records. But it seemed to be closed."

"The *mairie* closed in 2028. During the second pandemic. Never opened again. This village is almost dead."

"Elle s'appelait comment?" said the first voice. *"La femme que vous cherchez?"*

"Marie Vance."

There was a silence of unrecognition.

"Claire? Tu connais le nom Marie Vance?" one of the men called toward the bar.

"Non, ça ne me dit rien," came the reply. "You could try the cemetery. It fell into disuse decades ago. But you could look amongst the gravestones."

Cyrus felt the barmaid approaching the table with a waft of nicotine and feminine sweat.

The barmaid said, "We have a lot of old photos if you want to look. Salvaged from the *mairie* before it closed." She left, and Haydn shuffled into the booth next to him with a clink of bottles. He placed both hands around the ice-cold glass. The barmaid returned a few moments later, and Haydn moved their beers so she could place something on the table. He could smell its dust and dampness.

"It's a box of photos," said Haydn.

"Who is she, this Marie Vance?" asked the barmaid, as she began rifling through the photos.

Cyrus didn't see the harm in explaining. "She was an American woman who built a mansion on the edge of this mountain in the 1900s. It was destroyed in the earthquake of 1915, and we believe that afterwards she may have lived here until she died."

"American? My mother told me there was an American woman who hid Jewish children during the war."

"Ah, La Borgne, oui. Avec le cache-oeil," said one of the men.

"The One-Eyed Lady," Cyrus translated for Haydn. "With an eye patch. And Lydia's eye was wounded in the Battle of Ypres."

There were some nods of recognition and mutters about La Borgne, as they remembered the local legend. They explained that she had lived in a manor house not far from the square, and it was still there, but was a ruin. And there were comments about how La Borgne had not been mentioned for years; the vagaries of chance, the commonplace heroes who are forgotten. Cyrus translated all this for Haydn, aware of the double irony of a blind man looking for a picture of a woman of unknown appearance, with a girl who didn't speak French. He let the villagers' nostalgic chatter wash over him. He could hear rummaging amongst the photographs, the blur of fingers on the table as everyone dived in.

"Regarde," came the voice of the barmaid.

Haydn said, "The lady is showing me a framed photo of a woman and a group of children." Her voice was strange. "I haven't seen her before, and yet...I have."

"Describe it to me."

"She is tall and strong, plain, angular face, an eye patch, and wearing farming clothes—boots, breeches, short-sleeved."

"Did your mother tell you anything else about this American woman?" Cyrus asked the barmaid.

"Not really. Only that this village was known for its activities during the Resistance, in the Second World War. Many heroes. There is a memorial statue in the cemetery."

"Do you think it's possible she is listed on it?" asked Haydn.

"It's worth a look," he said. "I keep doing that. I can't look, can I. You keep searching through the photos. I'll listen to what they're saying."

Haydn was very quiet, evidently still looking at the photo.

"Where have you seen her before?" he asked.

"I haven't. In real life, I mean. I haven't seen that face. I don't know that person. And yet I have such a strong feeling of *déjà vu*."

"One doesn't really know one's own face. It's always a surprise when one looks in the mirror."

"Are you saying I'm looking in the mirror?"

He knew that Haydn was starting to realize something, and he felt there was little time left to leave things unspoken. "Tell me. What are you starting to realize?"

"You tell me."

"I will wait for you to tell me." He reached out and put his hand on hers. He then turned back to the men. "Of course, it was long before your grandparents were born, but did anyone here ever talk about the earthquake of 1915?"

"Only that it left the ground unstable and polluted," said one. "It exposed the sulphur springs that were within the mountain —made it unliveable, poisonous, especially near the edge of the village." He motioned in the direction of the cliff edge. "Ultimately, it led to the decline of the village. Most people left."

"Nothing about a castle that was destroyed, that fell into the gorge?"

"*Non, rien.*"

"We thought we might go there," Cyrus ventured.

"You can't go into the gorge," said the barmaid. "There's no way down, and it's toxic."

"Not necessarily into the gorge. We thought of going past the village to the top of the mountain, to the edge of the fault."

"You can't go there either. The road is blocked, and there's a perimeter fence, electric, barbed wire. A few years ago, someone tried—a hiker. I remember him because he stayed here at the *auberge* overnight. We warned him, but he wouldn't see reason. One of those urban explorers."

"What are they saying?" whispered Haydn. Cyrus translated as quickly as he could without missing the next piece of information.

"Anyway, it turned out he was reported missing, and a few weeks later his body was found not far from the fence. I can't remember if he was electrocuted by the fence or if he fell through some unstable ground."

There was some discussion about how exactly he died, and Cyrus interrupted with, "Can you remember which year that was?"

"I can," said the barmaid. "It was 2018. March 2018. I know because that's the year I got married."

"*Deux mille dix-huit,*" repeated Haydn. "That means 2018? I was born in November 2018."

The barmaid handed them baguettes filled with cheese. They had not asked for anything, and this gesture was a gruff, calm acceptance that they were welcome. After saying their goodbyes, they ventured out into the heat of the day to visit the manor house. It was behind the main street of the town, only a few footsteps away.

"This must be it," said Haydn, describing it to him. "Set back from the road, a large front garden and a swathe of land behind. A jumble of outbuildings and extensions. It would have been relatively easy to hide people here."

"Does anyone live here now?"

"Oh no, Cyrus, it's a complete ruin. I doubt anyone has lived here in more than fifty years, maybe longer."

"The whole town seems to be a ruin."

"What did you make of the people in the *auberge?*"

"The last of their kind."

"Perhaps they would have acted differently if they thought we were going to try and access the cliff edge."

"We are."

"Yes, but not in that way. We're not going to do what that hiker did. We're going to leave the village, drive to the bridge across the gorge, and send in a drone."

Every time she said the word *drone*, his heart beat faster. Were they really going to do it? "I don't know why," he said, "but I have a feeling those locals wouldn't have encouraged that idea either. There was a sort of—not quite fear—but more an acceptance that 'our world ends here, and that place is not for us.' Do you know what I mean?"

"Maybe. What I feel most is a strange sense that I've been here before. Even though I know I haven't."

"That's what Daphne felt. She didn't admit to me that she hadn't been here before; why would I have believed her? Well, I didn't believe her anyway."

They lingered in front of the house in the blazing sun. Cyrus was tired and short of breath, but he felt there was no option to rest now. They must see this through.

"The cemetery is just over there. Can you make it?"

"Yes, yes, don't fuss, I'm blind, not an invalid."

They walked to the cemetery, her arm in his, Cyrus stopping every few moments to mop his brow with a handkerchief and catch his breath. Haydn creaked open an iron gate, signalling they had arrived.

"The war memorial is right here at the entrance," she said, placing him so that the fronts of his feet were touching stone. "It's a stepped plinth up to a stone cross, and there are bronze plaques all around it with names." He could hear her clambering up to the plaques, whispering names under her breath. But there was no mention of a Marie Vance; only male names were listed.

Haydn found him a bench in the shade of a tree. He could smell the sweet scent of the needles of a yew tree, the tree of death. He could make out the shadows of headstones.

"I'll go and look..." A few minutes later, she called, "Cyrus, I found it!"

"Bring me to it," he called, noticing the crack in his voice.

She led him down the gravel path, into a shady corner.

"It's unkempt and forgotten, but there's no doubt. It says Marie Vance, 1880-1955, 'La Borgne' *Tante Bien-Aimée du Village.*"

"Beloved Aunt of the Village," he translated. "Can I touch it?"

She helped him to kneel, and he held the top of the gravestone for balance. He felt the lichen and cool, rough stone. His hand moved down until he felt the grooves of lettering, and he moved his fingers through the shape of "Marie." Suddenly, he convulsed with a sob and tried to disguise it as a cough. Daphne had no grave. Perhaps Lydia's was the closest he would get.

"Who decides?" he said, his voice cracked, as he slowly hoisted himself back to standing.

"Who decides what?" Haydn asked.

"The people who are remembered, and the people who are forgotten."

"So, Lydia didn't die. She lived until old age. We were rather quick to write her off. I imagined her having hurled herself off that cliff, following Seraphine's premonition."

"But she did keep Seraphine's ideals alive. She lived off the land, opened her house to the poor and vulnerable."

"Yes, that's true. Seraphine had a surprising influence on her. All those socialist ideas…communal living…and she did fill a house with children."

"Why did she not write any more letters to Jung?"

"Perhaps she did. What survives is so dictated by chance."

Come back to me, Cyrus, if you can.

CHAPTER 16

Cyrus

2035

They drove from Avenières to the bridge in slow silence. Haydn drove reverentially, taking each hairpin bend so slowly it felt motionless, as if the air was thick with resistance. There were no other cars on the road, the whole world seemingly in a state of limbo, as if they two, Haydn and Cyrus, were taking the last journey that would ever be taken. Cyrus thought of Lydia and how her letters had likened Seraphine to Persephone; Seraphine, who picked poppies and dreamed of death and bathed in the strange waters of a deep gorge. Seraphine, who gave her life to Lydia and never left the Chateau des Miroirs. He had a sudden stab of terror for Haydn, who was about to risk everything, about to dash herself against the rocks, for…for what? A chance at knowledge?

By the time they reached the bridge, it was late afternoon, and the lowering sun bathed them in the last of the day's warmth. They sat side by side on a bench at the edge of the bridge. It must have been close to where Cyrus and Daphne had stood with their binoculars, looking for the chateau. He felt he could sit on this bench for eternity. He felt that he probably would.

"I take it you can't see a house then?" he asked.

"No house. But it's so beautiful. The fault mirrors create these two kaleidoscopes, tunneling infinity into each cliff. And the valley is almost fluorescent green, rolling away across France. I'm sorry you can't see it."

"I have seen it, remember? When I was here in the 1980s, you couldn't hear the river or the birds. Just the drone from the motorway and airplanes in the sky. You don't hear that anymore."

"There are silver linings to the flight ban, then," said Haydn.

They listened to the cries of seagulls—an incongruous sound so far inland—and a raucous flock of starlings. Cyrus squinted up to try and make out the shapes against the sky, but all he could see was the floating sun shapes inside his eyelids. They listened until the birdsong seemed amplified, ominous. He wanted to say something about augurs, something about Roman mythology, but Haydn spoke first.

"Tell me what Daphne described when she told you what she saw—what else?"

Images emerged through the fog of his memories. "A fairy-tale castle, a cliff edge, a woman wearing an Edwardian dress. She had red hair and a white dress, and she was laughing."

"And dancing, right?"

"I...maybe." His vision was so enmeshed with Lydia's letters that he didn't know whose memory was whose, and whether any of it was real.

"There's something I have to tell you, Professor."

His heart lurched.

"I had visions, too. Almost the same as Daphne. I was on the edge of a cliff, looking at a fairytale castle, and there was a woman with red hair, in a white dress, laughing and dancing, too close to the edge."

Cyrus frowned. "When did you have these visions? Before or after reading the letters?"

"I think I have always had the visions. I know what you're implying—that I read these letters and put myself into the story somehow. But it's more than that. It's like a madness. No…it was too real for that. And I knew it was here. I always knew I had to come here. It was like the future reaching back into the past, telling me to come. With Daphne, it was the past calling to her… With me, it was something slightly different."

"And what is your theory? I know you have one."

"You tell me, Professor. I know you have a theory about my theory."

He took a deep breath. Once these words were said, they could not be taken back.

"You think that you were Seraphine in a past life. You have been reincarnated. That's why you dye your hair red."

She paused, and he waited patiently for her to formulate her thoughts. Urgency meant little now.

"You were correct," she said finally, "until around two hours ago, when I saw that photograph of Lydia. I saw myself in her eyes. All this time, I thought I was Seraphine, but the vision I have of the girl with the red hair—that's me, inside Lydia, looking at Seraphine. I am Lydia."

Cyrus knew that Haydn had turned to look at him, imploring him, and he couldn't bring himself to say what he still could not admit. More words still unspoken. He couldn't bear it. Perhaps if he were to cling to philosophy. If…then… logical assumptions.

"Listen," said Haydn, as if reading his thoughts. "Marie Vance died in 1955. What year was Daphne born?"

"1955."

"And when did she die?"

"1980."

"That hiker who went to Cruseilles and fell into the gorge—he died in 2018. That's the year I was born. We can speculate that he was born in 1980. Daphne. The hiker. Haydn. Lydia. And beyond."

"So, you're saying that Daphne, this hiker, and you are all reincarnations of Lydia, all trying to get back to Seraphine?"

"Yes, that's what I am saying. Like we discussed in your lecture on souls. Quantum physics makes reincarnation possible, believable."

Here they were, at the edge of all things, daring each other to believe.

"Let's say," he said, "for the sake of argument, that reincarnation exists. Then, if all souls are reincarnations, new forms of particles flung out from the beginning of the universe, what is so special about this place? Why do you, and previous incarnations of you, keep being drawn back here? Why isn't everyone in the world desperately yearning for something?"

"Well, I think everyone is desperately yearning for something. Isn't that what Lydia said? Where would we be without yearning? That is what drives humanity. But there's something different that happened with Lydia and Seraphine. Something…"

"Don't say magical."

"I wasn't going to. Improbable. Against the odds. And yet there are always odds. Cyrus, do you know what a monopole is?"

"Yes, vaguely," he said, the vision of Roy Lightman looming large in his mind. Always there, somehow. Roy Lightman and his theory that monopoles were two halves of a whole, trying to find each other out there in the universe, *like two lost souls*. "They are particles that have only one charge. Very rare since they were created with the Big Bang and since then have been flung into the corners of the universe. Correct?"

Haydn said, "Yes, basically. I like to think of souls as monopoles, two halves of a whole. Separated at the birth of the universe and desperately searching that universe for their other half. But the other half is almost impossible to find. No one really knows what would happen if two monopoles of opposing poles collided. But there would likely be a huge, unlimited release of energy. And those particles could never really be torn apart."

"It's like a metaphor for human yearning. Always searching for one's soulmate. That's what magnetism is."

"Yes, soulmate, exactly. But it's more than a metaphor. Lydia and Seraphine were soulmates, two halves of a whole, united by a miracle. It hardly ever happens, but it did. Then the house fell, and became trapped outside of time. And when they were torn apart, Lydia kept searching for Seraphine, even in her next life. Seraphine is still here, somehow. Drawing us in."

Cyrus smiled. "It's a very pretty analogy."

"I'm rolling my eyes, Professor, just so you know. It's more than an analogy, and you know it. The fact that quantum physics is ripe with metaphor is not just coincidence. We are grasping at something just out of reach, some other way of seeing the world. Can't you see that?"

"Perhaps we are not meant to know." He felt so close to the edge of knowledge, to the edge of death.

"We have already discovered things we are not meant to know."

There was no birdsong now, only an eerie silence. Or was that a faint rumble in the distance? The lowering sun was darkening the shadow behind his eyelids.

"Who are you, Haydn?"

"Like I said, first, I thought I was Seraphine. Now I believe I was Lydia. Then Daphne. Then, whoever that man was. And now…"

"That's not what I mean. I know you are not a student at the university. And yet people seemed to know you. I don't believe you are the great-great niece of Carl Jung. So, how did you get those letters?"

"Some of those things are true; some are not. My father was related to Carl Jung. That is not a lie. My mother was Korean. We lived for a time in Switzerland. And among the boxes in the attic, I found these letters. When I was very young. So, I always knew this story. Then I came across your Disappearing House problem…"

"How?"

"When I was a teenager. I would search for stories—legends, true crime, urban mysteries, movies—about houses that disappear. And I found a video of one of your lectures. The Disappearing House Problem. I realized immediately it was the story from my letters. It sounded so familiar. I couldn't let it go. I built it up in my mind over time that you would be the one to solve my problem."

"Did you ever think that maybe you just read the letters when you were very young, and so they became a part of you, like a lucid dream? You got confused between dreams and reality?"

"Of course. But it's so strong."

"Yes. I understand. Daphne knew she hadn't lived it, but she also knew it wasn't a dream. And she was so convinced, she was prepared to give up everything."

"And then my parents died, and it was impossible for me to go to university—no money. But I found my way to Oxford, and I got a job at the Physics Department. As a lab assistant for Professor Lightman. Well, I just walked into your college every day that I wasn't working, and then walked into your classes. If you look conspicuous enough, nonchalant enough, nobody questions you. People have other concerns these days, so you can hide in plain sight. Could you try to believe that it's true?"

"But this is the problem I have. Can it be a coincidence that you found the letters, and you are so connected to the person in the letters? Perhaps anyone who found those letters could have put themselves into the story."

"I don't know if I believe in coincidence," she said. "And I know you don't want to call it synchronicity."

Cyrus sighed. "Ah, synchronicity. Jung and his scarab beetle. The gift that keeps on giving."

"Well, that's what my great-great-uncle would have called it. But since that's not good enough for you, let's call it retrocausality. If time is not linear, then the future influences the past as much as the past influences the future. I find the letters, and therefore, I am the reincarnation of Lydia. My story is happening in parallel with hers, with Daphne's, with future versions of us. Joined by invisible threads, mirror shards of time reflected in each other."

"Retrocausality." He leaned back, stretched out his legs, and crossed his arms. As if posture alone could dilute the surreal gravity of their conversation. "A terrifying thought. That someone from the future could be reaching back and influencing us. The same someone who wiped the house from historical record, I suppose."

"They might not necessarily have bad intentions."

"Well, whoever it is, they are doing a rather bad job at the moment, I fear."

Somewhere in the distance, the rumble was unmistakable now. Cyrus felt a slight chill invading the warm air, as if something had been sucked into another part of the atmosphere.

"It might not be a someone. More like a something. Those silver threads, tying worlds together." She took the drone out of her backpack. He could make out its shape, hear the clicks and whirs as she prepared it. He feared it the way he would fear a weapon, a gun.

"So, are we going to look, before the sun goes down?"

"It's up to you, Professor. I always wanted you to decide for me."

He hoisted himself to sit upright again. "Let's go through it again. Like philosophers. If Daphne did manage to reach the house in 1980, and it was in superposition, she would have collapsed the waveform herself. Into one of infinite possibilities, the probabilities of which we are unable to calculate. If she…if she didn't make it to the house…then the house is still waiting to be observed. We have the means to look at it."

"Just because you can, doesn't mean you should."

"I think you have encapsulated all of human history, my dear. And since we may be coming to the end of history, and since the human Promethean quest for knowledge has always triumphed over restraint, I believe we are going to look. At some version."

"And which version do you want, Cyrus? Is there any version of this that could make you happy?"

"I want the truth."

"I do too. But truth is a kaleidoscope. A trick mirror."

The drone soared across the gorge, a strange mechanical wasp. Haydn felt the curious vertigo of watching the screen roll and dip between her maneuvering thumbs as she piloted the console. She hovered the drone for a moment and turned it to look at the dark reflection of the little flying machine, a tiny speck in the fault mirror. When the drone reached the edge of the opposing cliff, Haydn paused again for a moment, hovered, took a deep breath, and pushed her left thumb forward to move the joystick. There was a momentary resistance, a glitch on the screen, and then the drone seemed to suddenly speed up, as if it had passed through some invisible wall of resistance. The image flickered with interference, and then the drone was soaring towards a house. The house from Haydn's vision, from Lydia's letters. Except it was a ruin.

The Chateau des Miroirs was perched on the edge of the cliff. A little more erosion and it would go crashing into the void. It was gangrenous, the brickwork like rotted flesh, eaten away by time. There were pockets of infestations of flies. Some of the windows were broken, and Haydn saw a gap through which the drone could be maneuvered into the house. Enough light piercing through holes in the roof for her to make out a once-grand room, littered with shards of mirror. A chamois looked at the drone, then galloped off through a doorway.

There was a goshawk's nest in the open grand piano, mice running along the floor between the shards.

At the large round table, there were figures—corpses. Their skulls grinned fiendishly, as if they had died smiling. Two skeletons wore moth-eaten taffeta gowns, there were two in men's suits, and one with a South Asian-looking tunic. He held the bony hand of a woman in a white linen dress. Around her neck was a scarab pendant.

As if from far away, underwater, Haydn heard Cyrus's voice.

"Tell me what you see."

But she could not speak, because to speak would be to betray the tears streaming down her face.

"Tell me what you see." More forcefully, urgently, his voice cracking.

"I see her. I see Daphne. She is smiling. Wearing a white dress, dancing in the garden. She looks beautiful, Cyrus. She is alive."

It didn't feel like a lie, or even a kindness. Just a description of another reality, another possible world. What was the difference? What did it matter now? It wasn't difficult to imagine other worlds, because she had been imagining it all along. And there were so many other things they would never be able to see. Not with their eyes. And no matter how many mirrors were put into space, no matter how powerful the microscopes and magnets that were built, there were some things that would never be seen or comprehended.

Haydn felt his right hand move towards her, trembling, and she put her left on top of his, entwining their fingers as some small comfort. They sat for a long time, until she felt the hand grow colder and colder.

In the distance, a siren. Then another, and another, dissonant choirs of warning echoing over the mountains. She would have to move soon, because her story was not over.

An Archivist; a being of light, or a silver thread entwined with infinite others—or if we wish to make him human—a being wearing all white, sitting in front of a large bank of screens, carefully transferring control back to Haydn's drone screen. The fabricated footage of the ruined chateau is removed and seamlessly transferred back to the gorge. Haydn sees one possibility, the best possibility for her to see and to describe to Cyrus. The real house remains a secret, as a silver thread reaches into the past, or the present, or the future.

Haydn does not see the real house; she sees a ruin. Because Haydn will go on believing in the march of time, in human strife. And Cyrus will die believing that Daphne is free and happy, because Haydn is kind. These are the archives of the past, present, and future. These are the Akashic records. It is not for us to say who or what the Archivists are. And it is not for us to say whether they are sinister, or benevolent, or both. It is not for us to decide.

They are the Lords of Light, or they are spiritual beings, or they are fundamental forces of nature.

Two souls colliding is a chain reaction inside an atom that contains the whole universe.

Because secrecy is a part of history.

Because there are some things we are not meant to know.

Because without the yearning that mortality brings, we are nothing.

Because the threads will never break. And the cycles must keep repeating, as we keep repeating our mistakes.

242

CHAPTER 17

Daphne

1980

Daphne felt a gradual change in the atmosphere as she climbed. It was not due to altitude; it was not particularly high, by Alpine standards, and she was moving slowly. And the air did not feel thinner, quite the opposite. But she felt an almost imperceptible magnetic pull, not in one direction but shimmering through her. A weight, pulsing around her and inside her flesh like some sonic frequency too low to hear. Something unearthly. She kept thinking of strobe lighting, even though she could not see it. But when she closed her eyes, her retinas were alive, and she could see innumerable flashes through her veins and capillaries. She felt she had come within range of some strange, invisible cocoon. As if there was too much gravity here.

She looked up, squinting into the late afternoon sun, and saw a falcon soaring against the blue. It was barely moving, perhaps borne by some thermal that gave just the right amount of resistance to simulate immobility. But no, its wings were moving backwards, in contrary motion, and it was flying in reverse. It was rewinding, ever so slowly. She shook herself. No, she was mistaken. It was moving forward after all. But how strange that the sun was not setting. And should it not have moved across the sky by now? How long had she been climbing? This was like a lucid dream, one of those dreams where you can never seem to arrive where you want to go.

On her rocky perch, she turned to face the mountain. She saw the motionless shadow of a bee, clumps of poppies that moved the wrong way in the wind.

Finally, at the top, she hauled herself over the edge, and the house loomed up behind. The light was blinding; it was more than sunlight. The first thing she saw was herself, waving a warning. It was her, a version of her, telling herself not to come. But how could she see herself? And then that version of herself disappeared. On the stone steps were a group of figures dressed in white. They moved with ease but very slowly, in slow motion, a painting brought to life, a movie played at half-speed.

A beautiful red-haired woman stood up as if she had seen a ghost.

"It's you. But oh God, why did you come here?"

It was her, the woman from behind her eyes, and it answered every question that should never have been asked. For a moment, time stopped, and the world was her, and she was the world.

The red-haired woman came toward her, and Daphne had the curious sensation, a horror, that she was moving both slowly and quickly. It took her forever and no time at all to rise and move the few meters from the stone steps to where she was. They looked into each other's eyes for a fraction of a second and forever, and then Seraphine took her hand and led her towards the house. Again, it took them forever and no time at all to reach the threshold.

Seraphine took her inside the house, and in the hall she reeled, mouth half-open, as she understood, without it needing to be explained to her, that there was no time here. In the ballroom, moving images were everywhere, an infinite kaleidoscope. The two fault mirrors on either cliff face were eternal palimpsests revealing everything that had ever happened or would happen all at once, and all reflected from the mirrors inside the house. Daphne saw the rays of light passing through the pale emerald eyes of Seraphine's stained-glass image in the giant window.

What is this place, she asked, yet she didn't speak, because it was not necessary to speak since all was already known, including thoughts.

We call it Nowhen, Seraphine smiled. And did that smile last for a second, or a whole year?

She was one of the keepers of time now. She was omniscient. There was no time, so there was no purpose. Each mirror was a shard of time, a vision of a moment. A moving image captured, with the serenity of unmeaning.

And Daphne saw that perfect knowledge was worse than no knowledge.

She saw an exploding star, sucked into a vortex; a medieval battlefield strewn with bloodied, armored corpses; a herd of bison; two lovers in a dappled forest; the parabola of a nuclear missile; a crowded playground; the trundling carts and sparkles of a diamond mine.

She saw tracks in the snow, waves crashing on a beach, her own birth. She saw a woman dancing in a red dress, on a gold disc. A young, bereaved Cyrus, frantically looking for her in

Avenières. A gray-haired woman holding a red box filled with Post-It notes. Two women walking arm in arm in the Tuileries, one holding a cane. An elderly man and woman walking down Oxford High Street, the man with a cane. A white figure striding across grass in a college quadrangle, a white figure manipulating time. The manifold moments that make up the familiar flux of everyday life, the surge of progress, no longer unfolded for her like a piece of music, no longer reached forward like an arrow, but presented themselves all at once. All connected by silver threads that wound between the four dimensions of the universe, weaving together sense and chaos. Some immense machine that turned with wheels of infinite complexity.

She was no longer looking out of time; she was looking at time, from the outside. Here she was at Nowhen, where forever was the same as never. She had found her twin soul for eternity, except that eternity meant nothing, or it meant hell.

She contemplated the full horror of this eternity; an ouroboros, an endless cycle of repeated mistakes. She would now carry the weight of longevity, carry the weight of oceans and literature, of seasons and empires turned to dust. She felt the vertigo of forever.

Time was a God, and that God had lied.

CHAPTER 18

Haydn

2055

Swirling black flakes in the fog settle on the charred remains of cities, skeletal structures of monstrous masonry half-crumbled to their foundations. Frozen rivers of melted asphalt meander in between, while black rivers flow viscous through the scorched earth. Time moves differently here, in this nuclear winter. But the world continues to turn, and somewhere up there still burns the sun.

Beneath the ruinscape, Haydn Young, Keeper of Memories for Bunker 27aCH, perches on an ancient charred wooden desk. Her legs dangle like a girl, despite her graying temples. She finishes telling her tale to the room of students that sit on a ragged assortment of chairs and cushions. Strip lighting casts shadows on the concrete walls and flickers according to the vagaries of the generator. "There you have it. The Letters Of Lydia Temple. Thoughts? Forget whether it is true. What do we learn from this tale?"

Her group of students shifts positions, rifle through their notes, and whisper to each other. Then a few hands are raised.

"It's a metaphor for the downfall of the old European order. A palace of excess on the edge of a cliff, built pre-First World War, that collapses into the abyss."

"It's a late feminist attempt to co-opt Jung's ideas and claim he took them from a woman."

"It's the treatment for a movie called The Possibility of a House."

"The house built on the edge of an earthquake-prone cliff symbolizes the risk of nuclear war—built on flimsy foundations, based on a mistaken belief in the fundamental goodness of people."

"The house is a metaphor for the consequences of technology—the mirror shows the dark side, the shadow house."

"The whole thing is a metaphor for time."

"It's a philosophical teaching tool."

"Could it have been created by Carl Jung, as a case study?"

"The professor's blindness is a metaphor for the limits of human perception."

"Daphne climbing the cliff represents the Sisyphean human struggle to claw free will from destiny."

"It's a philosophical explanation of free will within a deterministic universe. Each human is a quantum being with free will, doing their own thing; the human race as a whole is probabilistic."

"The mirrors—it's about mirrors. In psychology, the hall of mirrors signifies that the patient is delusional and confused. So, it's a metaphor—what is real, and what is illusion?"

"It's a metaphor for women's history being erased by men. The house was built by women's ingenuity, labor, and engineering. And yet it has disappeared. All the ideas of the men in the story were prefigured by women."

"It's Cyrus hallucinating. There's a condition whereby people who have recently gone blind formulate bogus experiences in their minds. Charles Bonnet Syndrome."

"Lydia is a metaphor for unconditional love. The love we all aspire to. It's about never giving up. If Cyrus had only allowed himself to love the way that Lydia loved, then maybe… Perhaps Lydia is who we should all aspire to be."

Haydn, who has been leaning back on her palms to enjoy the responses, shifts into an upright position and smiles. "That's getting close."

Another hand is raised, from the back of the class. A man with red hair and pale emerald eyes. On his uniform is the emblem of the scarab, the emblem they all wear in bunker 27aCH.

"It's a true story," he says.

She smiles. "Now we're getting somewhere."

After the class files out into the corridors of vast caverns, Haydn turns off the lamps and arranges the chairs. The man with the red hair and pale emerald eyes has stayed behind. They approach each other, accelerating, smiling, then fall into each other's arms, entwined like DNA.

And out there in the caverns, above there amongst the ruins, the endless cycle continues.

❧

Acknowledgments

I am so grateful to Cassandra L. Thompson and the team at Quill & Crow Publishing House; for your professionalism, energy and support, and for continuing to believe in my writing. I am very proud to be a Quill & Crow author.

Thank you to Mathew L Reyes for your invaluable comments and advice on the manuscript.

And thank you again to the readers. It means the world to me that people take the time to read my work, and I hope that The Fault Mirror has given you something to take away with you.

- Catherine Fearns, 2025

About the Author

Catherine Fearns is a writer and musician from Liverpool, UK. Her Amazon-bestselling *Reprobation* series of crime fiction novels is published by Northodox Press, and her first historical fiction novel, *All The Parts Of The Soul*, was released in October 2023 by Quill & Crow Publishing House. She has also been widely published as a music journalist, specializing in heavy metal. As a composer her sheet music is published by Universal Edition, and her solo albums released on Blue Spiral Records. She has four children and lives in Geneva.

Other Books by Catherine Fearns
All the Parts of the Soul
Buried Lightning (forthcoming)

Thank you for reading *The Fault Mirror*. We deeply appreciate our readers, and are grateful for everyone who takes the time to leave us a review. If you're interested, please visit our website to find review links. Your reviews help small presses and indie authors thrive, and we appreciate your support.

Other Titles by Quill & Crow

The Bone Drenched Woods, L.V. Russell

All the Parts of the Soul, Catherine Fearns

Welcome to Meadowbrook, Cassandra L. Thompson

9 781967 911042